"Why fight it?"
Julian murmured.

"Fight what?" Kelly asked.

"The magic."

She stared at him, trying not to sink into his hypnotist's gaze. "I don't believe in magic," she said.

"No? But it's in you," he answered softly. "There's all kinds of magic. There's the kind that men create, and then there's the special magic one can find only in a woman's eyes..."

Breathless, she gazed up at him, feeling the spell of his seductive, probing gaze radiate through her, as his warm hand slowly slid from the small of her back to her shoulders.

"There's powerful magic in your eyes, Kelly," he whispered.

A sensual shiver pulsed through her as his fingers grazed the back of her neck, playing with the damp tendrils of hair. Ever so slowly, he bent his face to hers. Her upturned face tilted, as if magnetically drawn, to receive his kiss...

Other books by *Lee Williams*

Second Chance at Love
STARFIRE #189
PILLOW TALK #216

To Have and to Hold
HOME FIRES #43

Lee Williams, *who also writes songs and scores for musicals, lives in New York City's Greenwich Village. Although she enjoys the bright lights of the city, she's most content at home with her husband and cats, cooking up desserts of her own invention.*

Dear Reader:

February is a good month for romance — not only because Valentine's Day falls on the fourteenth, but also because in so much of the country, freezing temperatures and snowy blasts make you want to snuggle up with someone you love. And when you're not curling close, you can read SECOND CHANCE AT LOVE romances! They, too, are guaranteed to keep you toasty warm and wonderfully satisfied.

We begin the month with *Notorious* (#244) by Karen Keast. Many of you wrote in to compliment Karen on the superb job she did on her first book, *Suddenly the Magic* (#255, October 1984). In *Notorious* she's written a boldly sensual variation on *The Taming of the Shrew*, except in this case veterinarian Kate Hollister sets out to domesticate decadent playboy photographer Drew Cambridge — once she realizes she can't resist him, that is! You'll love watching Kate transform this devil-may-care womanizer into a perfect lover . . . and husband!

Have you ever wondered how magicians bend keys and saw people in half? These intriguing secrets — and more! — are revealed in Lee Williams's most original, riveting romance yet — *Under His Spell* (#245). A phony psychic, a sleek, slobbering leopard, and sexy, black-garbed magician Julian Sharpe make *Under His Spell* an unforgettable romance with a *very* magic touch.

We were pleased and impressed with Carole Buck's first romance for us, *Encore* (#219, September 1984). Now *Intruder's Kiss* (#246) establishes her as one of our brightest talents. I love the opening: Sara Edwards, armed with a squash racquet, is about to tackle two noisy intruders — who turn out to be a huge sheep dog and charming, devastating Matt Michaels. Although wildly attracted to Matt (not the dog!), Sara begins to wonder: Just who *is* Matt Michaels? You'll be delightfully entertained by this lively, sexy, fun-filled tale.

Few writers capture the sizzling chemistry between a hero and heroine better than Elissa Curry. In *Lady Be Good*

(#247), she creates two truly unique characters: Etiquette columnist Grace Barrett is poised and polished, perfectly coiffed and regally mannered; Luke "the Laser" Lazurnovich is an ex-football player who pretends to be even more uncouth than he really is. To tell how this ill-matched pair comes to realize they're perfect for each other, Elissa combines a delicious sense of humor with the endearing tenderness of an emotionally involving love story.

In her outstanding debut, *Sparring Partners* (#177, February 1984), Lauren Fox immediately established herself as a master of witty dialogue. Now, very much in the Lauren Fox tradition, comes *A Clash of Wills* (#248), which pits calm, controlled stockbroker Carrie Carstairs against outrageous, impulsive, infuriatingly stubborn investor/inventor Harlen Matthews. As you can imagine, they're an explosive combination. *A Clash of Wills* is wonderfully fresh and inventive.

You'll be *Swept Away* by our last February SECOND CHANCE AT LOVE romance, #249 by Jacqueline Topaz. "Cleaning woman" Paula Ward has dusted Tom Clinton's penthouse and is "borrowing" his lavish bathroom to prepare for a date, when the devastating millionaire arrives home — with guests! To save her job, Paula impulsively agrees to pose as Tom's wife — with funny, sad, and, above all, sensuous results . . .

February's SECOND CHANCE AT LOVE romances are sure to chase away your winter blahs. So enjoy them — and keep warm!

With best wishes,

Ellen Edwards

Ellen Edwards, Senior Editor
SECOND CHANCE AT LOVE
The Berkley Publishing Group
200 Madison Avenue
New York, N.Y. 10016

UNDER HIS SPELL
LEE WILLIAMS

SECOND CHANCE AT LOVE BOOK

***a special thanks to
Lora, Tedrich
and Howard H.***

UNDER HIS SPELL

Copyright © 1985 by Lee Williams

All rights reserved. No part of this publication may be reproduced or transmitted in any form or by any means, electronic or mechanical, including photocopy, recording, or any information storage and retrieval system, without permission in writing from the publisher.

Requests for permission to make copies of any part of the work should be mailed to: Permissions, Second Chance at Love, The Berkley Publishing Group, 200 Madison Avenue, New York, NY 10016.

First edition published February 1985

First printing

"Second Chance at Love" and the butterfly emblem are trademarks belonging to Jove Publications, Inc.

Printed in the United States of America

Second Chance at Love books are published by
The Berkley Publishing Group
200 Madison Avenue, New York, NY 10016

Chapter 1

AT HALF PAST FIVE one Tuesday afternoon in June, Kelly Robbins was still at her desk. The Walkman tape recorder at her side was turned up to full volume. She was so immersed in trying to decipher her interview with an astrophysicist, conducted in a crowded bar the week before, that she almost didn't hear the noise from the doorway through the din in her headphones. Then it came again, louder.

A growl.

Kelly looked up. There was a leopard standing in the doorway.

Kelly's blood froze. The leopard's tail twitched from side to side. Female and feline regarded each other, with only a few yards and a desk between them.

The leopard studied her, its orange-gold eyes gleaming, wide black nose quivering. For a suspended moment of sheer terror, Kelly remained frozen in her seat. Only her mind whirred into action, at hyperspeed.

Scream.
Don't scream.
Move.
Don't move.
Drop behind the desk, slowly?
Dash for the closet, quickly?
Throw something.
Throw up.

As she watched, the leopard lowered its sleek, furry head and advanced toward her desk. Kelly stiffened, drawing back against her chair. Her heart pounded and seemed to be lodged in her throat. She stared helplessly at the approaching beast.

The incongruous melange of conversational chatter and jukebox music in her ears abruptly ceased as the tape reached the end of one side.

Kelly watched the awesomely sinewed muscles ripple beneath the animal's spotted pelt. A sudden flurry of absurd questions whizzed through her panicked brain.

Was her brand-new Giorgio Armani cotton shirt about to be ruined, horrifically shredded by massive claws that cared not a whit for fashion? Shouldn't her life be passing before her eyes? Was she more likely to survive a jump through the window behind her and a fall of thirty stories... and if not, who would finish the interview she was writing up?

The leopard had paused, half its menacing face hidden beneath the desk. All of a sudden it rose, front paws resting on the desktop. Kelly gasped. Her head snapped back. Her neck muscles—every muscle in her body—ached with the strain of trying to propel herself back. She'd have pushed herself through the chair if it were possible.

There was something in the animal's mouth.

She stared in disbelief as the leopard opened wide its jaw and dropped a mangled wad of glossy paper on her desk. Her own jaw fell open slowly as she recognized her name on an uncreased portion of the topmost sheet and realized what the leopard had been chewing.

It was an article ripped from the current issue of *Omnibus*. Her article—on Wolfgang Lang, the German psychic.

The leopard licked its spittle-covered lips and growled.

But a leopard that read *Omnibus* wasn't likely to attack her. In fact, a leopard that had tried to eat her article had most likely been sent in to frighten her... as a gag? A gag pulled by someone like—

Albert. Her managing editor hadn't liked the story, and nearly killed it at the last minute, backing off only when two senior editors rallied to the piece's defense. The rotund, balding middle-aged wise guy was known for his hyperbolic gestures. Was this his way of getting even?

The leopard bared its teeth menacingly, and pushed the mangled magazine pages across the desk with its paw.

But Kelly was at last capable of breathing, and she exhaled a deep breath. No longer as intimidated, she slipped the lightweight headphones off her ears. Clasping both hands behind her neck, she leaned back in her chair.

"Well," she said, and cleared her throat. "It seems like *everybody's* a critic these days."

The leopard licked its lips.

Even though her heartbeat still thundered in her ears, Kelly continued to affect total relaxation. If Albert was waiting outside to see her come flying out of the office, hysterical, or collapsed behind the desk in a dead faint, she wasn't going to give him the satisfaction. The giant cat was obviously tame... wasn't it? It must be.

"A leopard that reads our magazine might be good for publicity, though," she told the beast. "What can I do for you?"

"That depends."

Kelly looked up. The man standing in the doorway was tall, tanned, and rivetingly handsome. His gaze was piercingly direct—dark eyes gleaming beneath dark bushy eyebrows—and his face had a formidable air. Kelly took in his well-groomed mustache, square jaw, thick black hair curled rakishly over his forehead.

"Who are you?" she asked.

The man ignored her question. Both he and the leopard appraised her in silence. Kelly imagined she could palpably feel the man's eyes flickering over her face and figure like little laser beams.

"You're not what I expected." His voice was a caressing rumble that resonated from deep within his broad chest.

She stared at him. "I could say the same for you and your... friend, here," she said. "Where's Albert?"

"Albert?" He looked at her blankly. "Who's Albert?"

The leopard growled again, and Kelly looked back at it with growing alarm. "You mean..." she began, as the adrenaline started pumping furiously once more. "He is— yours," she managed. "Isn't he?"

The man was still standing in the doorway as if he had all the time in the world, studying her with those luminous eyes of his. Kelly's gaze swung quickly to the gleam of metal in his hand: a chain leash and collar.

"Look," she said, indicating the equally watchful beast hovering at the desk. "Do you mind—?"

The man shrugged. "You look so comfortable, sitting there," he said, with the hint of a smile on his face. "I'd expected a scream, at least."

"Sorry," she said tersely.

He was, at last, sauntering slowly up to the desk. "And I had the impression you'd be . . . older."

"Who sent you here?"

"Nobody."

"Why are you here?"

"To introduce myself."

By way of jungle beast? Who *was* this character?

He was easily over six feet tall. He towered above her, and as he put a hand casually around the leopard's shoulder, the ferocious-looking beast seemed to diminish suddenly in stature, and appeared docile.

He was openly examining her now. His deep brown eyes traveled from her reddish-blond hair, cut fashionably short, to her ocean-green eyes, her slim pert nose, past her full lips and the smooth curve of her chin to her long neck— and the cleavage amply visible from his higher vantage point, revealed beneath her partially unbuttoned shirt.

Kelly felt some color returning to her blanched face. As the leopard was now licking the man's hand, she felt it safe to move again. She pulled her shirt closed, smoothed a lock of hair back from over one eye, and pushed herself, and the chair, farther from the desk.

"Put a leash on it," she suggested, evenly. "Or I'll have to call security. How did you get in here, anyway?"

He looked at her with amusement radiating from the velvet depths of those magnetic eyes. "Maybe I walked through walls." He shrugged. "You'd believe that, wouldn't you?"

Kelly narrowed her eyes at him. "What's that supposed to mean?"

The man picked up the wad of magazine paper by one

sodden tip and dangled it in front of her briefly before dropping it on the desk again.

"You fell for Wolfgang Lang's mumbo-jumbo," he said. "I imagine I could persuade you I had powers like his, too."

The leopard was now nudging her crystal paperweight around with its nose, a little growling noise coming from its stomach. Too indignant at this man's brazen invasion to be frightened anymore, she snatched the object out of the leopard's range and reached for the phone.

"Wolfgang Lang phoned before he came, at least," she said. "But seeing as you don't have an appointment, and you refuse to collar your pet—"

"Down, Sig," the man said quietly. The leopard immediately dropped from the desktop to the man's side. In one smooth motion the man fastened a collar around the animal's neck, and with a jiggle of the chain had the oversized feline lying obediently on its stomach.

Kelly held off on calling security, and folded her arms. "Look, Mr.—" she began.

"Sharpe. Julian Sharpe."

The name had a vaguely familiar ring. "Mr. Sharpe, if you've got a beef about the article I wrote, you'd be better off writing to the editor. Getting my attention with some... circus animal... may have been your idea of fun, but I'm—"

"He's not from the circus," Julian interrupted smoothly. "And I'm not interested in letters to the editor. You're the one I want to talk to." He cocked his head, and he seemed to be measuring her, trying to figure her out. "You know, when I started reading that article I was really rooting for you. Here's somebody who's got both feet on the ground, I said to myself—she'll see right through this bogus charlatan... and that's why I was so disappointed when he pulled the rug out from under you in the home stretch. Although," he added, a sensual gleam appearing in his eyes, "I'm far from disappointed to be meeting you. Most intellectuals don't look like you do."

Kelly searched the man's face for signs of deliberate mockery. She found none, but realized her heart was doing an unaccountable flip-flop as Julian Sharpe returned her gaze. His eyes expressed a lively interest as they held hers, and the corners of his mustache turned up in the hint of a smile. There was something downright bewitching about his face. He reminded her of a buccaneer, or a pirate, or some dashing figure from a more romantic era. She forced herself to look away.

The leopard was apparently dozing on the carpet, at Julian's feet. His head rested on his paws, eyes shut, and only his slowly swaying tail gave any indication of animation.

"Then this isn't a practical joke?"

Julian's face darkened. "Not at all," he said. "What I have to talk to you about is completely serious." However attractive he was, the man could evince an air that was downright forbidding.

"You always take your pet leopard out for a stroll this time of day, then?" she asked dryly, holding her own.

"Let's just say I found an indirect way of expressing . . . dissatisfaction," he replied. "And a direct way of getting your undivided attention."

"All right." She sighed. "You've got it. So, shoot."

"May I have a seat?"

Kelly glanced at the leopard. "Well, *he's* made himself at home."

Julian chuckled. "He senses you're not afraid, so he's relaxed. That's unusual, with strangers." There was a trace of admiration in his voice.

"How'd you get past reception with him?"

Julian's eyes twinkled mischievously. "Trick of the trade."

"Which is?"

"I'm a professional illusionist, Ms. Robbins. Maybe you've heard of me, and my brother—J and J Sharpe?"

"The magicians," she said, remembering now that she'd seen posters advertising their show plastered around the city. So that accounted for the man's provocatively mysterious air! He was an entertainer, that was all. "I see. You've been performing here. And the leopard—"

"Siegfried works with us," he said, nodding. "We've

Under His Spell

just finished up a tour by playing the Palladium."

Kelly looked him over more carefully. He was dressed in predominately black clothing: black slacks that hugged his hips tight and outlined lean, muscular legs; a black knit cotton sweater with two bold painter's stripes of red and mauve across it. The sleeves were rolled up and she noted the fine hair covering his strong forearms. A devastatingly good-looking man, with powerful presence. But what an odd profession—he seemed too bright to jibe with her idea of a top-hatted, cane-twirling, show-biz type performing glorified parlor games. The depth she sensed when she looked into his eyes seemed to signify there was... more to him than that.

"Well, Mr. Sharpe, you've got an original way of publicizing yourself, but I don't see what you want with me. The article I wrote wasn't about magic—it was about parapsychology. And *Omnibus* isn't interested in doing another—"

"I'm not interested in publicity," Julian interrupted coolly. "We've just finished a very successful tour, with all the coverage a top-of-the-line act could expect. I'm interested in the truth. Your article *was* about magic—pure chicanery in the first—or lowest—degree. Wolfgang Lang is nothing but a fake."

Kelly stared at Julian, which required looking up, even though they both were standing. At five feet, five inches, she was used to being shorter than most of the men she knew. In heels, she was still dwarfed by the imposing "illusionist," but nonetheless she affected her most commanding air, thrusting out her chin defiantly.

"If you read my article carefully, Mr. Sharpe, you'd know that there's a great deal of evidence to support Lang's possessing genuine psychic powers."

"Hogwash," Julian said pleasantly, shaking his head. "Dr. Roberts, John Simon, that lunatic from Hofstead University—what do they know?"

"They're scientists," Kelly said hotly.

"Exactly," replied Julian. "Ever heard the expression about trying to catch a thief?"

"I try to avoid clichés in my line of work."

"The point is," he went on, unperturbed, "you don't use a scientist to expose a magician. He doesn't know what to look for."

"Hold it," Kelly protested. "I wasn't out to expose a magician. What I did was interview and profile a world-famous psychic from Germany on the eve of his first visit to America. I did my research, and I started out skeptical—until I saw the man perform the impossible with my own two eyes. Then I wrote up my impressions. And if you ask me, I did a damn good job. The man barely speaks English!"

"You did too good a job," he retorted. "Now all of your readers are going to believe as you did—that Lang's the genuine article."

"Listen," she said, beginning to bristle at the man's arrogance. "If you want to take it up with Dr. Roberts and Dr. Simon, who haven't been able to explain away the man's powers and certainly seem qualified to do so, go right ahead. But I'm already working on another piece—which is what I would be doing if I hadn't been rudely interrupted by you and that pet of yours."

Siegfried looked up at her balefully, then closed his eyes, head resting on his paws.

"He'd make a good office fixture if he was stuffed, but alive he's just a nuisance," she finished, hands on her hips.

Julian Sharpe gazed at her in silence, shaking his head. "You're a smart, savvy lady," he said. "You've obviously got a lot on the ball to be an associate editor for a magazine like this, at your age. If you've been duped, don't you want to know about it?"

Kelly sighed. "Shouldn't you be off sawing someone in half, or something? I have a lot of work to do."

Julian squinted at her, then smiled. He bent forward across the desk, his face suddenly even with hers. Kelly was startled by his unexpected closeness, and his laughing, glinting eyes. But though she mentally commanded herself to step back, her body didn't listen.

"Kelly Robbins," he murmured, his velvety deep voice

Under His Spell

somehow making the simple pronouncement of her name a seductive flirtation. "Your Irish contrariness is showing. And so is your New England stubborn streak."

She stared at him, momentarily mesmerized. How on earth did he know...? Well, her name, of course, but..."I didn't realize my accent still showed," she said.

"Enough," he admitted. "Maine, isn't it?"

She was all too conscious of a tingling awareness in her body of his very masculine presence. As she leaned both palms on the desktop, she caught a clean, strong scent of minty soap and a musky after shave.

"What of it?" she said.

"Just curious," he replied, his voice husky and low.

"If you have any other questions," she began, "you can..."

"Put them in the mail? I'd rather not."

"Take it up with the people at Hofstead," she suggested.

"I'd rather take things up with you."

"I'm not interested in...things."

"No?" His smile was deliberately suggestive.

This conversation was rapidly veering off the track and into dangerous territory, but Kelly couldn't bring herself to break away. The velvet brown depths of Julian's eyes were sensuously inviting. He was devastatingly handsome. Her heart was beating faster again.

"Mr. Sharpe—"

"Julian."

"—there's really nothing to be gained by talking to me."

He raised one bushy eyebrow. "You're too self-critical."

"What I mean is," she began, coloring, "now that you've had your fun, and you've expressed your opinion in such a...an effective, if adolescent, fashion, you'd be well advised to take your—"

"Where'd you learn to talk like that?" he interrupted. "Journalism school?"

"All right, Sharpe." She glowered. "Get your ass out of here. And take your furry friend with you. Is that plain enough English?"

"Indeed," he said, eyes twinkling. But instead of moving

away from the desk, he eased one leg over the edge of it. Half sitting, half standing, he folded his arms, his smile an invitation to a showdown.

"You know," she said coolly, "I'm liking you less and less by the minute."

"Funny," he replied. "I'm liking you more and more."

"Then do us both a favor and remove yourself, before I have to embarrass you by providing a uniformed escort."

"You're pretty good with leopards, Kelly. Don't tell me you're afraid of a mere man."

Kelly glared at him. He seemed to be enjoying himself immensely at her expense. She'd met some smug, slick entertainers in her line of work, but this guy was . . . something else. Beneath his good looks and blatantly sexual aura was a layer of sheer bedrock self-confidence that galled her. She wasn't used to being so blatantly confronted.

"I'm serious, Mr. Sharpe. You can bait me all you want—while we wait for security to get here."

She reached for the telephone.

The shock of his skin against hers stopped her even more effectively than the gentle but firm grip around her wrist. Her fingers hovered helplessly a few inches above the phone receiver. She could feel her blood pounding beneath his strong, smooth fingers as she stared at him, too startled to struggle.

"Let go of me," she commanded.

"There's something I don't understand," he said conversationally, still gripping her wrist. "You're a journalist—a reporter of sorts. If there's another side to the story you haven't yet heard, why are you turning a deaf ear? Your professional interest should be aroused."

"I don't like being strong-armed," she said pointedly.

"Fair enough," he said, nodding, and he let go of her, then added; "Or are you afraid your professional reputation will be tarnished if I'm right?"

Her skin was still tingling where he'd touched her. Kelly rested her hand on the phone, wavering. That was a challenge if she'd ever heard one, and he knew—didn't he?—that she'd have to rise to it.

"All right, Mr. Sharpe. What evidence have you got? How can you substantiate these accusations of yours?"

"Now we're getting somewhere." He stroked his mustache with the side of his thumb, considering. "I'll tell you what. In your article, you described Wolfgang bending a metal key without using physical force—by sheer psychic energy. Is that correct?"

"Right before my eyes," she told him.

"Was anyone else there?"

Kelly considered. "Steve Lipman, a staff photographer. And Fritz Murnau—you know, his translator-assistant—"

"Right, right," Julian said impatiently, rising from the desk. "Fritz is always there. Before, during, and after..." He frowned, and then his gaze alighted on the extra chair she kept in the little space behind her office door. "Ah, that's good."

As Julian strode across the room and pulled the chair out, Kelly tried to reason away the surge of curiosity she felt watching his tall, rangy form in action. The man had some primitive, animal magnetism that couldn't be ignored. Man and leopard didn't seem such an unlikely pair; Julian was as lithe and graceful in his movements as Siegfried, who yawned when she glanced at him, exhibiting an awesome display of gargantuan molars.

"I'll bend some metal for you," Julian announced, setting the chair up directly opposite her. Siegfried rolled over, his upraised paws an absurd echo of a domestic kitten's playful pose. Julian ruffled the fur on the big cat's belly, then settled into the chair, which was a simple metal frame with black cushions. "Sit down," he told her. Then he added, reacting to the look in Kelly's eye, "Please."

Kelly sat slowly in her own leather chair. Seated, she was still beneath Julian's eye level, a fact that annoyed her. "Well?" she asked. "What now?"

"I'm going to perform a feat of otherworldly psychic power," the magician informed her, intoning the words with an edge of sarcasm.

"You mean a trick? What's the point?"

"The main difference between a professional conjurer

like me and a deceiving faker like Wolfgang Lang is a matter of pretensions," Julian said. "I'm going to do for you just what he did, but I'm not going to pretend I have fantastic gifts. Give me a key."

Kelly reached below the desk for her handbag. She withdrew from it her ring of keys and examined them, deliberating. Wolfgang had bent one of Steve's office keys into a curved "U" shape that had rendered it useless. If this Sharpe character was really capable of doing something similar, she was wary of using a key she needed.

"Let me look," he said, and swiftly relieved her of the keys before she could protest. "Tell me," he murmured, as he examined each key, "did he do this in broad daylight?"

"No," she remembered. "He had Steve turn the bright floods off because it interfered with his concentration. What are you—?"

He had selected a key from her chain and held it up, then reached over to turn on her desk lamp. He pulled its shade toward him so that his chest and lower face were highlighted in direct glare from the bulb. The overhead fluorescents were still on, humming quietly.

"Now I'm in plenty of bright light, yes? And there's nothing up my sleeves," he noted, indicating his rolled-up sweater. "I'm as close to you now as he was, aren't I? It was described that way in your article."

"Yes," she said, and her eye was involuntarily drawn to the soggy, crumpled-up papers on the desktop nearby. Julian leaned forward and swept them aside, placing the remaining linked keys at her elbow.

"Now," he pronounced, sitting up straight. "He held the key like so?" He held it up from the pointed end, enclosing most of it in his hand. Kelly nodded. "And he concentrated..." Julian made a show of furrowing his brow, as if great effort was being expended. It was, Kelly had to admit, a good imitation of the German psychic's posture and attitude.

"He rubbed the key, too," she prompted.

"Oh, yes," murmured Julian. Key still held tightly in his

Under His Spell

fist, he used his thumb to stroke the topmost part of the key. "And then?"

"He held it up closer to his forehead," she told him. Julian complied. "Then he concentrated harder—" Julian shut his eyes tightly, brow still furrowed. "And then, as he rubbed it—"

"Look," Julian interrupted. "It's going."

Kelly's mouth dropped open. The key was bending. Julian's fingers weren't moving and the pressure of his hand seemed barely perceptible beneath her wide-eyed scrutiny. The key was now drooping forward at a forty-five-degree angle. "My God," she whispered. "That's just..."

"What Wolfgang did," Julian finished, opening his hand. In the middle of his palm, Kelly's brass key lay, two-thirds of its long stem folded over like an L-shaped piece of licorice.

"No," she muttered, shaking her head in disbelief. "You couldn't have..."

"With sheer psychic brain power? No, you're right. I used force."

Kelly stared at him, bewildered. Her mind was whirling back to Wolfgang's seemingly spooky supernatural feat, comparing it with the same act just performed right under her nose in bright light—and somehow even more unbelievable. "But your hand wasn't moving," she murmured. "At least, I didn't see..."

"You didn't see," he repeated, nodding, and dropped the key on the desk. He straightened her lampshade so the glare no longer shone at him, and sat back in the chair, looking smug. "You saw your key—straight, unbent—then you saw me hold it in my hand—" She nodded. "And you saw me concentrate until the key bent, apparently of its own volition—or, if one was foolish enough to believe such malarky, from the force of my magical brain waves."

Kelly cleared her throat, looking down at the bent key. "What you didn't see," Julian went on, "was my taking your key and jamming it against the metal frame of this chair." Kelly stared at him. "All I needed was a moment, which I got by distracting your attention"—Julian leaned forward, pushing her keychain even closer to her elbow—"and with my other hand below your line of vision, I bent the key against the chair." He straightened up again, cupping the bent key in his palm. He held it up as he had moments before.

"You mean, it's already bent when you show it to me," she said slowly.

Julian nodded. "And it looks straight when it's concealed in my palm. Then all I have to do is move the key forward a bit at a time..." He demonstrated. Once again, the key appeared to bend before her eyes. "And *voilà!* A miracle." He smiled at Kelly's look of chagrin. "Any sleight-of-hand artist with a strong wrist could bend a key after practice."

"But—" Her belief in her own powers of perception was crumbling. "But the other things he did—"

"I can do." Julian rose from his chair. "I'll match that charlatan down the line." He lifted the chair easily and replaced it by the door.

"How do you know he used the same method? Just because you can duplicate—"

"I'm sure he does," Julian said confidently. "I've seen him in action. And I've been conjuring and studying the art of it all my life. Anything Wolfgang Lang can do, I can duplicate." He faced her again, that arrogant, roguish smile on his face. "But Lang's no dummy," he went on. "He loves journalists, because they're so susceptible—no offense," he added. "But he won't let a professional magician within a mile of him. That's why I need you."

"Me?" she repeated, startled.

"I want to expose Lang for what he is. And you can help me do it." He smiled. "You're perfect." He was sizing her up again with his eyes.

"But... why?" she asked.

"Well, you've got a keen mind," he began. "And I'm sure you can be seductively charming when you want to be, so if you asked for another interview, you could—"

"No, no," she interrupted him, trying to ignore the sensuous warmth his gaze was radiating. "I mean, why expose him? What's in it for you?"

Julian paused. She sensed him assessing, editing, carefully forming his reply. "I'm proud of my profession," he said simply. "Wolfgang Lang is a disgrace to the craft I practice. If he was claiming to be a great entertainer, I wouldn't care—I might even respect him. But he's claiming to be a genuine psychic, with extraordinary spiritual, superhuman powers. A man like that's dangerous. Accrediting him discredits some of the best scientific minds in this country."

A magician with a social conscience? Julian Sharpe seemed to take himself, and his craft, very seriously. Kelly looked at him, perplexed. Her mind was trying to comprehend many things at once, while her spirits were in danger of sagging. The article on Lang had been her biggest coup at *Omnibus*, earning her the admiration of the staff and her grudging promotion by Albert Hill to associate editor after only two years on staff. Now this self-assured cape-and-wand wielder wanted to turn her victory into an ignominious defeat. And she was supposed to help him make her the laughingstock of the magazine world?

"I'll admit that I may have been hoodwinked," she said slowly, each word painful for her to enunciate. "But I don't see where I—"

"Good for you," he said, with a quiet forcefulness devoid of sarcasm. "A lot of other journalists in your position would be too embarrassed to admit they'd been duped—after they'd bought Lang's act."

"I haven't bought yours yet," Kelly said wryly. His accolade registered inside her with a little tingle, as sincerely given. Julian Sharpe's directness did have its disarming side. "And even if I were convinced that Lang was a fake," she went on, "it's not the policy of *Omnibus* to do follow-up stories, as a rule. The most we could do is print an editorial retraction."

"And leave your winsome face with pie all over it?" His eyes twinkled. "No, I'll go you one better—and much bigger. Lang's embarking on a tour of the U.S. now. You know about his ultimate destination?"

"The Halliford Institute," she replied. "In California."

"Right—where he's going to be subjected to supposedly rigorous tests under so-called foolproof conditions, and where he undoubtedly plans to confound American scientists who won't know how to deal properly with an expert conjurer. Now, if we can show him up for what he really is, you've got an important story—an exposé of the pseudo-science of parapsychology that could really shake up scientific academia."

Kelly had gotten to where she was, in part, by thinking on her feet. Julian Sharpe was suggesting a way to turn a potential disaster into another coup, and she immediately grasped the possibilities. "You mean, cover the tour," she mused aloud. "Then after the Halliford testing..."

"Reveal how he's hoaxed America," Julian finished. "With my inside knowledge and your journalistic flair, we could make quite a team."

Team? The idea of her hooking up with this strange breed of showman who looked like a pirate struck her as preposterous. But there *was* a story here...

Siegfried rose, chain jingling, and sat back on his haunches at his master's side. Both looked at Kelly expectantly. Once again, she felt a surge of indefinable agitation as she met the man's eyes. The open sensuality in his gaze made her stomach flutter.

"So you say you can do everything Wolfgang Lang can do."

"Absolutely."

"Would you be willing to demonstrate your... abilities here, at this office, with a number of people present?"

"I'd love to."

He continued to hold her eyes with his, and Kelly felt a warm flush of arousal at the undisguised provocation she saw in them.

"Let me sleep on it," she said at last, having the queasy feeling she might be making a big mistake.

"And if I demonstrate my abilities for you satisfactorily?"

His mustache was curling upward again. The man had the knack of imbuing any remark with an unmistakably sexual subtext.

"Then I'll see if we're interested in taking things further."

"I like the sound of that," he said, his smile broadening. "I would like to take things further."

"I'm sure," Kelly said dryly. "But I'm not the one who makes final decisions here."

Julian's eyes narrowed. "You mean, someone makes your decisions for you? How old-fashioned."

Kelly sighed. "I answer to an editor—one among others. Many people have a say in what stories we choose to do."

Julian nodded absently, as if thinking of something else. His eyes were taking a leisurely tour of her face and figure. "I'll call you then," he said, "in the morning."

"Why don't I call you?"

He shook his head. "I can't be reached at any particular number." Abruptly, he stuck out his hand. "A pleasure to meet you."

Kelly shook his hand and had to repress a shiver as his warm, smooth skin encased hers. Silently, she endured the gentle, titillating squeezing of his powerful palm, then pulled away.

"Sig," Julian commanded quietly, and the leopard rose, following him to the door. Julian paused in the doorway, turning back. "Honestly," he said, his voice teasing, "I'm amazed he fooled you."

"Wolfgang was very personable," she said, defensive. "He seemed trustworthy."

"Yeah," said Julian. "I'm surprised he didn't lift your watch."

Kelly glanced at her wrist, then gasped.

"Here you go," said Julian. Her digital wristwatch dangled from his outstretched hand. "Sorry." He smiled. "Couldn't resist."

Lips set tightly together, Kelly came out from behind her desk. She was wary of approaching Siegfried without a desk between them, but she was also determined not to show a trace of fear. She stopped a few feet from Julian. He handed her the watch.

"Thanks," she said. The leopard was sniffing at her ankles. She stood rooted to the carpet, inwardly flinching as the big beast's whiskers tickled her stockinged calf.

"You're welcome," Julian said. He didn't move, but observed Siegfried's careful inspection of her legs. "I think he really likes you," he noted.

"How nice," said Kelly. She could feel the leopard's warm breath.

"He's got good taste." Julian smiled and gave the leopard's chain a tug. "See you," he called jauntily, walking into the hall. Siegfried followed.

Kelly stood where she was for a moment, till her heartbeat slowed, then returned to her desk and sat down. Quickly she pocketed her bent key and swept the crumpled *Omnibus* article into her wastebasket.

Any hopes of resuming her tape listening were dashed. The day was shot, if not the week—if not her career. Since Albert believed he'd done her a great favor by hiring her in the first place, he derived pleasure from making her job as difficult as possible. If Julian was right, and she'd been hyped and duped, she would never hear the end of it. Damn that man and his oversized feline!

A thunderclap jarred her from her reverie. Glancing at the window behind her, she could see that the dusk outside had darkened into a gloomily gray storm-to-be. Great—a perfect capper; she had, of course, brought no umbrella.

Hurriedly, Kelly got her things together, grabbing her orange, smocklike cotton gauze coat from behind the door, and turning out the lights in her little office.

Most of the other offices off the corridor were dark. As was usual since her ascent to associate editor, she was the last to leave—or almost. Biff, the art editor, was still huddled over his giant white drafting table in the art room as she whizzed by and called out a good-bye.

The elevator appeared just as she did, in the hall outside their suite. Kelly ran over and squeezed in as the doors shut.

Everyone else was dressed, as she was, for warm spring weather, and all wore expressions of annoyance and trepidation at the approaching storm.

The area by the glass doors of the lobby was filled with various other office people staring glumly at the street. Rain was pelting against the pavement in torrential sheets.

Kelly briefly considered waiting inside for the deluge to abate. But as another flash of lightning illuminated the lobby, quickly followed by a resounding peal of thunder, she was seized with a sudden rage of impatience.

What the hell! In this weather, at this time, in midtown Manhattan it would be impossible to find a taxi. Her apartment was within walking—or running—distance, just a dozen blocks uptown. She might as well brave it.

Her coat was soaked through by the time she reached the end of the block and her hair was a sodden mass of curls. Somehow it seemed only appropriate to be stalking resolutely through a massive downpour—a fitting end to a miserable day.

Drenched to the bone, shivering, Kelly waded her way uptown. Occasional pedestrians sprinted by with essentially useless newspapers shoved over their heads. She didn't bother to run. She could change when she got home.

As she walked, her mind's eye kept picturing that arrogantly aggressive but undeniably attractive man who'd showed her up as a fool... and had somehow managed to be gentlemanly about it. She couldn't quite get a fix on Julian Sharpe. Definitely not the superficial type, and yet he made his living in such an unorthodox, seemingly frivolous way... She felt there was more to him than met the eye, but on the other hand, what did meet the eye was so alluring as to suggest a lady-killing nature. A man who was sort of like...

Richard.

Kelly allowed herself a grim smile of self-awareness. So—that was who he reminded her of; that accounted for her instinctive attraction to his magnetic physicality, in all likelihood. Old love-'em-and-leave-'em Richard, the dark prince of broken hearts.

Did she have some neurotic blind spot where tall men with mustaches were concerned? Odd, wasn't it, that blond-haired Doug from *We* magazine didn't do a thing for her; that brown-haired Lewis from Random House hadn't exactly set her heart aflame—but a man with jet-black hair and a mustache sauntered into her office and—zing!—the chords were struck.

Kelly shook her head, pausing at a corner long enough for a passing bus to splash her skirt and stockings. Not a tragedy—she was already soaked from head to foot. She pushed onward, thinking of a warm bath, her cotton robe, some soothing music, a hot dinner...

...Richard, that dashing weasel, had captured her heart with his soulful eyes and poetic words, only to trounce it as vigorously as his long, powerful fingers had pounded the keys of a piano. Their romance had been passionate at first. Initially, his I-won't-grow-up, charming boyishness had been immensely attractive. And she'd been willing to put up with his ever-wandering musician's life. When he was there—in between the late-night sessions and the out-of-town gigs—he was all hers. But then she began to realize that the words *commitment* and *responsibility* just weren't in Richard's vocabulary. And all her love might not be enough...

The final revelation, after talk of marriage and many a separation followed by romantic, rapturous reunions, had nearly destroyed her. It turned out that, along with some of the out-of-town performances, Richard enjoyed in-the-sack dalliances—affairs that he considered too "unimportant" to threaten his relationship with Kelly. They just happened, he said. Well, she just happened to be old-fashioned about such things. Though he promised to stop his philanderings, the damage done by this breach of trust was irreparable, and she was out the door—miserable, but much matured.

Kelly sighed. Over, she recited, as the rain beat down; done; *finis*. Why dwell on it? It was only seeing that handsome—what had he said?—"illusionist" that had stirred up some long-repressed feelings. She was probably best off staying far beyond the range of his practiced hypnotic gaze.

At last, her block was in sight. As Kelly turned the corner

of Second Avenue and began to pick up speed, dying now for dryness and warmth, she heard a heart-rending sound that stopped her in her tracks: the forlorn mewling of a cat caught in the rain.

Where had it come from? Kelly squinted, bent down, then spied the soaked, shivering animal, hardly bigger than a kitten, piteously meowing as it clung to the bottom step of her building's stoop. The tabby feline's coat wasn't dirty and ragged; it wasn't an alley cat, but most probably belonged to someone in the building who'd carelessly let it slip out.

The cat reminded her of the stray she'd adopted back in Maine when she was a kid. "Here, kitty," she murmured, and coaxed the poor thing into her arms.

Then she ran up the steps to the front door of the little brownstone apartment house, hurriedly digging into her handbag for her keys as the tiny cat clung to her, still wailing.

There was the keychain, but where—?

Oh, no. Oh, Lord, no.

With a groan. Kelly dug her trembling hand into the pocket of her soggy, clinging skirt.

Of course. It had to be the one he'd pick.

As another clap of thunder seemed to signal an increase in the force of the relentless downpour, Kelly stared at the hopelessly twisted piece of metal, while a tiny puddle formed around it in the palm of her hand.

Chapter 2

SHE COULD HAVE laughed or cried, while the rain sheets beat down upon her defenseless head, but crying seemed more imminent. It was cold, with gusts of wind that seemed to go right through her drenched clothing. No key to the outside door meant no entrance to the building until someone else who lived there happened to come home.

There wasn't even any overhanging porch to protect her at the top of the steps. Kelly quickly reviewed the little knowledge she had of the inhabitants' comings and goings at 234 East Sixty-seventh Street. There was a free-lance word processor—Harold—who was often leaving the building when she was coming home from work. Maybe he'd show. But then, she'd worked even later than usual...

Call the super, then, who was never there when needed. Well, she could wait in that overexpensive coffee shop on the corner of First, and drip all over the counter in between forays to the phone. How depressing. Why hadn't she waited for the storm to blow over? Right, Kelly, rub that misery in—why did you bother to get out of bed this morning?

The trembling cat yowled, digging its claws into her arm.

With a little groan of frustration, Kelly turned from the door and stepped into the puddle on the second step, filling the instep of her shoe with water. Muttering a curse, she continued down the steps.

"Kelly!"

Startled, she looked up to see someone waving at her, a tall dark shadow at the curb. Kelly blinked some water from her eyes.

"Well, don't just stand there looking like a water rat! Come on in!"

It was Julian Sharpe. He was standing at the opened door

Under His Spell

to what looked like a solid silver bus, parked by the curb. Impatiently, he waved her onward.

Ten minutes earlier, Kelly never could have imagined she'd be happy to see the man, but at the moment she was overjoyed. She dashed across the pavement to him and into the warm, dry safety of the bus.

"Welcome aboard," Julian said, closing the door behind her. He turned and, in the sudden quiet of the vehicle's interior, laughed softly at the sight of her, shivering at the top of the carpeted steps.

Kelly looked down, embarrassed. Already there was a puddle in the soft gray carpet at her feet. She knew she looked a total mess. There was water dripping from her soggy mass of hair, from her sleeves, from her shoes. Her shirt clung to her body; her gray skirt, soaked black, hung limply about her legs. The shivering kitten was trying to climb onto her shoulder.

Julian, as she glanced back at him, looked perfectly at ease, dry and...sexy, was her first thought. He'd changed into black-and-white tissue-weight linen drawstring pants that vividly outlined his perfectly formed legs. Good grief, she mentally admonished herself—how could you be admiring the man's legs at a time like this?

"I think you could use a towel," he said, that amused gleam in his dark eyes causing her to look away again.

"What are you doing here?" she asked him, moving aside as he bounded up the steps. She managed to extricate the cat and put it down on the floor.

Julian paused at her side. "I received some psychic emanations that a lady I knew was in danger of drowning," he said, with poker-faced gravity. "So I rematerialized myself in your vicinity."

"Cute," she said. At her feet, the cat shook itself and sneezed.

"You're the cute one," he called airily over his shoulder, headed down the bus's center aisle. "The wet look is very becoming on you."

Kelly watched him rummage about in an overhead compartment, and tried to keep her teeth from chattering as she took in the vehicle's interior. It was obviously a live-in trailer. The area Julian now stood in was compartmented off with a sliding door that hid the rest of it from view. He was leaning over a wooden table set in a black leather booth on one side of the carpeted aisle, and there were kitchen accoutrements on the other—counter, appliances, sink, and cupboards. The whole interior was done in unstained raw wood paneling and dark velvety material that gave it a rustic, homey air with a trace of refined, old-fashioned elegance.

"What is this thing?" she called.

Julian tossed her a fluffy white towel. "It's a 1947 Airstream trailer," he said. Squinting, he began pulling a brightly colored skein of cloth from the overhead compartment. "I'll see if I have a washcloth for your little friend," he murmured. But the piece of cloth was seemingly endless. As she watched, yard after yard of it appeared in a long pulley. Julian paused. "Stage handkerchief," he muttered. "I wondered where I'd left it..."

When she emerged from drying her hair with the soft, big towel, Julian was trying to stuff what looked like a mile of colored handkerchief back into the compartment, a bemused look on his face.

"You live in this trailer?" Gingerly, she removed her orange coat and held it out, dripping. Julian had found a smaller towel, which he handed to her now in exchange for the coat.

"I'll hang that up," he said, ignoring her question. Kelly knelt down and managed to give the little cat a quick rubdown with the towel before it dashed away, taking refuge under the driver's seat.

When she stood and turned, she saw Julian making space for her soaked coat in a narrow, two-foot-deep closet space near the door. She glimpsed various masculine apparel hung there, and some spangled and silver garments that were obviously clothes for the stage.

Turning back to her, Julian's eyes immediately riveted on her still-drenched figure. He had caught her in the act of lifting one arm to push back her hair and she realized her

Under His Spell

breasts were vividly outlined as they rose under her clinging shirt. She wore no bra.

"So this is where you live?" she repeated, awkwardly dropping her arm and then folding both arms across her chest, her eyes darting away from the undisguised interest in his look.

"Sometimes," he said.

She didn't need to be a journalist to note that when it came to personal questions, Julian Sharpe wasn't exactly loquacious. The silence that followed his reply was broken by the plaintive meow of the cat.

"I'll see if I have some milk for it," he said. "As for you..."

His voice trailed off. She could feel his eyes making a survey of her features. "Let's get you out of those clothes," he said abruptly.

"What?" Instinctively, she shrank away from him.

"Well, you're shivering and chattering and ruining the carpet," he said, and the twinkle in his eyes belied the apparent criticism inherent in that last remark. "And you obviously have no way of getting into your building at the moment. I've got a nice big, warm robe you could wear, and a heater in the back where you could dry those things off. Come on, I'll show you."

He made it sound like the most natural—and most innocent—thing in the world. Kelly looked at him, pausing in mid-stride down the aisle of the trailer, cocking his head back to look at her expectantly. His handsome, bronzed features gleamed in the soft light, and she was reminded, once again, of a pirate, somehow transported to twentieth-century Manhattan. Once more she felt that tickling tug of arousal in the pit of her stomach.

Mustaches, she reminded herself. That's all it is.

"It's not going to let up for a while," he said. The steady, gentle, but unbroken patter on the roof above her underlined his words.

"Lead on," she said resignedly.

She followed Julian to the sliding doors midway down

the aisle. He pulled them aside. Beyond them was a bedroom area, with a single but roomy platform bed on one side, a comfortable sofa on the other, and a little writing desk set into one wall beneath gray-tinted windows.

Off to one side, light spilled from an ajar door that obviously led to a small bathroom. Julian followed her gaze. "You can change in there," he suggested. "The robe's hanging on the back of the door. I'll get the heater out—it's stored under the bed."

For some reason her eyes were drawn to the bed. It was just a bed, an ordinary bed, much like the one she slept on in her little apartment, with its covers rumpled and pulled back just as hers probably were, upstairs. But she stared at it dumbly for a long moment before she became aware that Julian was watching her.

"It must be . . . different," she said, by way of explaining her sudden interest in his sleeping habits.

"Different?" His eyes held hers, the brown velvet depths warm and teasingly inviting.

"I mean, sleeping on wheels," she said, feeling a sudden flush of sensation flooding her body as his eyes exerted their not-so-subtle pull.

"It can be wonderful." His husky rumble of a voice was doing odd things to her sense of equilibrium.

"I'll just go in there and change," she announced.

"You do that," he said.

Left to their own devices by her distracted brain, her eyes had shifted to his mustache. Longer than Richard's, she noted, though not as bushy. As she watched, the full lips underneath curved upward in a seductive smile. Alarmed, Kelly tore her eyes away and stepped past him quickly to the bathroom.

Once the door was shut securely behind her, she stood staring at the strange, clownlike painting facing her on the wall. Julian Sharpe apparently had the power to awaken rapidly the most sensuous impulses of her psyche. The man might be dangerous . . .

She shook her head, as if to clear it, then gasped, horrified, as the clown in the painting did the same. It was no painted clown, but her own reflection in a mirror. She stepped closer, grimacing in dismay. Her makeup had run all over her face, the mascara leaving raccoonlike circles around her eyes and vertical lines down her cheeks like a mime might wear.

Kelly ran some hot water in the sink, soaped up her hands and then her face. Once it was cleaned of those grotesque smudges, she picked up a brush and attempted to make some kind of unfreakish sense of her toweled hair. Since it was cut short to just above her shoulders, making the disarray manageable didn't prove too difficult.

She unbuttoned her blouse slowly, eyes on the door, then realized she was probably being too paranoid. Quickly she slipped out of the soaked pleated skirt and rolled her pantyhose down. Stripped to her panties, which were wet as well, she debated whether or not she wanted the little blue-and-white-striped underpants subjected to Julian Sharpe's scrutiny. Shrugging, she slipped them off, deciding the physical discomfort outweighed the psychological.

The sensation of being stark naked with only a thin door between her and that magnetic magician, a scant few feet away, made a tight knot form in her stomach. Kelly reached for the robe, hanging where he'd said it would be, and quickly put it on. The robe, a comfortingly soft, warm maroon terry cloth, was much too big for her, but she belted it tightly and opened the door a crack, after a quick glance in the mirror assured her she looked basically presentable.

Julian didn't seem to be in the room. She opened the door wide. He'd set up an electrical heater by the desk opposite. Its coils were flaring orange as she watched, a gentle buzzing noise emanating from it as it warmed up. Kelly looked around her and approached the heater, her wet clothes in hand.

The desk was littered with silver objects she could only guess were tools of his trade, and piles of books and periodicals. Above the desk, on the black-velvet-covered wall, hung a portrait of a debonair-looking gentleman in a top hat that, if her memory served her well, was the legendary Houdini.

Kelly hung her skirt, shirt, stockings, and panties from the desktop, weighting them with the book piles, and aimed the heater on the floor directly at the bedraggled array of clothing. She heard Julian's voice murmuring something softly from outside, in the kitchen area. Curious, she quietly moved to the sliding doors and peered out.

Julian Sharpe was crouched on the floor. The cat sat in front of him, bright yellow eyes wide. A dish of milk lay untouched at its side, for its attention was distracted by the conjurer's hand. Julian was waving a silver chain in the air before the fascinated cat's face. As he moved his hand from left to right, the chain disappeared. The cat's face jerked, its paw arrested in midair. Julian moved his hand again. Magically the chain materialized. The cat turned again, mesmerized.

Kelly could see the magician's face in profile. He was smiling, and the look of pure, naïve enjoyment on his face did a funny thing to her insides. Crouching barefoot before his captive audience, totally enraptured in his little game, Julian had the sweet, innocent look of a young boy. Watching him at play in a world of his own devising, Kelly saw him unknowingly reveal a side of himself she'd never glimpsed before. She could picture him, suddenly, as he must have been in childhood, and she was touched by both his earnest absorption in the act, and his obvious affection for the fascinated animal.

He'd succeeded now in getting the cat to stand on its hind legs. It was poised there, paws raised, head cocked quizzically as its eyes searched for the disappearing sparkle of silver. Julian chuckled and flicked his wrist. The dish of milk rattled suddenly. The cat dropped to the ground. Cautiously, it padded to the dish, glanced, perplexed, at Julian, and then its little pink tongue flicked out to taste the milk.

As the cat began to lap in earnest, Julian rose. Kelly backed away from the half-opened sliding doors. Once more she was aware of how tall he loomed above her as he turned, hands on hips, to face her. The boyish face had disappeared. She was looking at a mature, commanding, and, she realized, well-guarded man.

He slid the doors open. "Goes well with your hair," he commented.

"Hmm?" She realized he was referring to the deep maroon of the robe. "Oh. I don't think I'll take it as it is, though," she joked, holding her hands out to show how the sleeve ends came down to her fingertips.

"Easily remedied." Julian stepped into the room, sliding the door half shut again behind him. He took hold of her hand and rolled back the cuff, doubling it up. She stiffened at his touch, mutely watching him roll up the other cuff and wondering how in the world she had allowed herself to end up in the man's portable bedroom with her clothes off. The rain was still quietly hammering on the roof. How long would she be captive here?

Julian let go of her hands and stepped past her, surveying her makeshift clothesline by the heater. "Shouldn't take too long to dry those." He nodded. "Now let's warm us up."

He knelt by a wooden cube that served as a side table for the sofa. With a tap of his knuckles, its front swung open on an unseen hinge. From its interior he extracted a bottle of brandy and two crystal glasses.

Kelly settled herself on the far end of the sofa, demurely covering her legs with the ample material of his robe. Its collar brushed her nose and she caught a whiff of an oddly familiar, musky-mint scent that she recognized as Julian's. Kelly pulled the collar down, made sure no untoward part of her anatomy was showing, and accepted the glass of brandy from Julian's outstretched hand.

He sat down on the opposite end of the sofa, stretching his long legs out, and raised his glass in a mock formal toast. "Here's to our joining forces."

"I'll drink to the possibility of it," she corrected him. "I haven't agreed to anything yet."

"Let's drink to being agreeable, then," he said.

"Fair enough." She shrugged. They both drank. The brandy was delicious, smooth and rich. It went down like silk and instantly began to blossom, a billowy warmth in her stomach.

"So," she said, after savoring the taste. "Maybe you'd

like to tell me now how you just happened to be passing by here."

Julian smiled. "You really think I 'just happened to be'?"

She shook her head. "But I know you didn't follow me home, so...?"

"I was on my way across town," he said, "when it occurred to me that one of your keys was out of commission. And since it was raining, and I happen to be a friendly sort of guy, I figured I'd better backtrack and help you out if you were stranded."

"How did you know where I lived?"

"Telepathy," he said, then winced at her blazing eyes. "Okay, okay." He grinned. "I looked it up. You don't have to be a magician to use the telephone directory."

Something about his explanation still sounded vaguely suspect to her, but she couldn't put her finger on it, so she let it stand. Taking another sip of brandy, she looked around her. There was a poster advertising the Sharpe Brothers framed on the wall by the bathroom door, dated some years back. The "Masters of Illusion" had been featured at an arena in Ohio.

"So now that your tour's over," she began casually, "you'll be heading back to the Midwest?"

He smiled, shaking his head. He wasn't taking the bait. "I'm enjoying it here. How about you, Kelly? How long have you been a New Yorker?"

He was good at this, the conversational turn-around. She had the feeling his adept avoidance of any personal inquiry was a product of many years of practice. But she had nothing to be secretive about. "Nearly eighteen years," she told him. "I like it fine."

He gave her an inquisitive look. "You must've still been a pipsqueak in pigtails when you moved here," he said, amused.

"I never wore pigtails," said Kelly dryly. "But I was young. Third grade."

"Must've been quite an adjustment for you to make."

You have no idea, she thought silently, as she shrugged. It had taken years—the first few, rather painful—to become "citified," bending over backward to unlearn her smalltown ways. By now she was so used to playing the metropolitan sophisticate that she could barely remember the early childhood she'd struggled so fiercely to put behind her.

"Don't you miss the countryside? Clean air? Open spaces?"

"Sometimes," she admitted. She followed Julian's gaze upward. And as she listened with him to the steady pitter-patter of the rain, she suddenly did remember something: the rain beating on the makeshift roof of the little tree hut in the ancient oak behind her house. She could almost smell that fresh, wet-earth smell the rain brought out. She closed her eyes, savoring it, remembering how she'd raced her older brothers through the fields outside of town in a summer storm like this one...

Julian was watching her. Kelly snapped out of her reverie. "Sure, I miss it," she smiled, self-conscious beneath his warm and steady gaze.

"I can see you," he said, eyes narrowing. "In a pair of cut-off jeans, dirty sneakers, and scraped knees... frog hunting. At the local pond."

"You can?" She laughed. "Do I look that much like a hick?"

"No," he said, smiling. "But without your makeup, it's easier to see the country girl underneath the cosmopolitan woman."

She didn't believe in mind-reading, but Julian Sharpe was pretty perceptive. His imagery wasn't that far off. Kelly shifted uneasily on the couch. Time to try the offensive tack again.

"So where do you hail from when you're not living on wheels?" He couldn't very well avoid an answer to a question that direct.

"Nebraska," he said, his faint smile acknowledging that he knew what she was up to.

"You grew up there?"

He nodded. "Near Omaha."

"And you still live there?" She'd hit a streak, and wasn't going to let up.

"Part of the year." He looked at her warily.

"On a farm?"

"I share some land there..."

"With your brother?"

Julian sat up, examining the copper liquid in his glass. "You're an inquisitive sort of woman, aren't you?"

"It's my job," she said. "You're a secretive sort of man."

"That's *my* job," he said, with a grin.

Silence. They both sipped their brandy. Kelly hid her own smile behind her glass. His grin was infectious. She was starting to warm up from the inside out. The heater, the brandy, and this man—who she couldn't help but notice was marvelously put together from head to foot— were having a significant effect on her.

Stick to business, she told herself. "Speaking of secrecy," she said, "I thought you people had some sort of code. How do you expect to expose Wolfgang Lang without giving away a magician's trade secrets?"

Julian nodded, swallowing a sip of brandy. "Yes, there is honor among conjurers. But some of Lang's tricks are so simple, any how-to beginner's magic book would yield answers to the curious. As for the more complex stuff..." He paused. "I'm willing to take *you* into my confidence," he said slowly. "And we can figure out together what to tell your readers."

Kelly studied him as he refilled her glass, then his. Already he was presupposing her cooperation, and implying he trusted her. But could she trust him? Then there was the research involved...

"You'd have to teach me many things," she posited, *"if* we were to work together."

"That would be a pleasure," he said.

Kelly felt herself coloring beneath his steady gaze. "What makes you so sure I'm the right person for you—to do this job?" she added quickly.

"You gave him good press," Julian said. "He thinks you're one of the faithful now. He'll never suspect you'll be acting as my eyes and ears, so his guard may be down..."

His eyes and ears. It had an alarmingly intimate sound.

"I don't know," she began. "The logistics involved..."

Julian nodded slowly, still holding her gaze. "We'll have to work very closely together," he said, his voice like a soft caress. Kelly forced herself to look away. The room wasn't swaying, but the brandy was definitely going to her head. She was the one being swayed, as the patter of raindrops continued, almost musical, above her, and the heater quietly purred close by. The little room was so cozy. Had Julian moved closer on the couch, or was her mind playing tricks?

Suddenly she was aware of another, unfamiliar sound: a kind of high, keening wheeze that was apparently emanating from the back end wall behind Julian. As she peered at it, the wall moved.

Only Julian's quick hand arrested her glass from falling from her grasp. "Wha-what's—?" she spluttered.

"Siegfried." He chuckled. "He's asleep behind there. I always pull that black tarp down so he can snore undisturbed by light or movement."

She could see now that what she'd mistaken for solid wall was indeed a rippling tarp. The back of the trailer was obviously at least another yard beyond it.

"I should've known," she muttered. Her heart was still pounding at a fast clip, though, and she realized it was because Julian was still holding her wrist with his hand. Take your hand away, then, suggested a liquor-lazied voice in her head. But she didn't. "You're quite a team, you and that beast," she said.

Julian leaned forward, his glimmering dark eyes now even with her own. "We could be," he said softly, his rumbling husky voice seeming to resonate right through her. "You and me."

His face was merely inches from hers, close enough for her to see the little soft smile lines at the edges of his eyes and mouth, and the sexy length of his eyelashes above those seductive eyes. The lips beneath his mustache were pursed invitingly.

Kelly felt the warm, slightly ticklish caress of his leg against hers, and a resounding sexual buzz seemed to spread from that point of contact through her lower regions and above. His fingers grazed the soft inside of her wrist, where her pulse pounded. His other hand had dropped to grasp gently at her hip beneath the folds of the robe.

Just as she was starting to lean forward, drawn by the hypnotic force of his simmering, sensual gaze, Kelly became aware that the robe had fallen open, revealing the soft mounds of her breasts. With a sudden start of modest self-consciousness, she straightened up, pulled the robe closed, and rose from the couch, her breathing fast and uneven.

"I—I think I should take a look up front," she said. "Someone might be coming in or out... of the building," she added, as he continued to look at her, the hint of a smile on his lips.

Abruptly, Kelly turned and left the little room, pushing through the sliding doors to the more well-lit kitchen area. When she reached the front door and was peering out through the side window, the glass of brandy still cradled against her chest, her heartbeat returned to a more normal pace. She realized that even if she were to spy someone entering or leaving her building, she couldn't very well run out of there, barefoot in a bathrobe, to stop them.

After a moment, she downed the rest of the brandy and deposited the glass in the little sink. When she returned to the bedroom, Julian was feeling the edges of her hanging skirt.

"Merely damp now," he commented.

"I think I'll brave the outside," she said. "It's not raining as hard, and if I make a few phone calls I can probably get in."

Julian straightened up, looking her over. Was there mockery in his eyes? Did he know how close she'd come to succumbing to his alluring powers of seduction? Hard to tell. She should know better than to have drinks with mustachioed strangers on an empty stomach.

"Suit yourself," he said pleasantly. Poker-faced, he handed her her panties, stockings, and shirt as she gathered up the skirt. She was about to reenter the little bathroom when a thought struck her.

"Say," she said, hand on the doorknob, "you didn't pur-

Under His Spell

posely bend my front-door key, did you? I mean, you couldn't possibly have known which one it was...?"

Julian looked at her blankly. "How could I know a thing like that?" he said, seemingly affronted. "And why would I purposely—"

"Skip it," she said, and quickly closed the door behind her. Just a crazy thought... but still, it occurred to her that a man like Julian Sharpe was not necessarily to be trusted. Sleeves or no sleeves, there was a strain of trickery in his nature.

The panties were toasty warm, the hose dry, and though both shirt and skirt were still damp and wet around the edges, she felt comfortable enough when she emerged.

Julian handed her her bag. "I'll get your coat," he said. She followed him into the kitchen, where the little tabby cat sat playing with Julian's silver chain. She scooped it up into her arms. Julian was at the front. "Still pretty wet," he said, handing her her coat.

Kelly shrugged, peering past him out the window. "Rain's letting up," she noted, and draped it over her arm. "I'm just going down the block to the phone..." She stopped, seeing the light in the first-floor apartment go on. "Great!" she exclaimed. "I don't need to phone. I can knock on Heidi's window. She's the woman who lives downstairs; she'll let me in."

She turned back to Julian, ready to say good-bye. The cat wriggled from her grasp. They both bent to catch it and nearly knocked heads. Julian laughed as the cat dug its claws into the upholstery of the driver's seat and glared at them defiantly.

Reaching past him to coax the cat, Kelly nearly lost her balance.

Julian caught her.

She leaned against him instinctively as she stood up, then started to move away. But his hand slid to the small of her back and she was trapped, looking up into his glimmering eyes.

"How about later?" he whispered.

"Later, what?"

"You and me."

"Here?" she said, a little dazed.

"Anywhere you like." He smiled.

"I'd like to go home," she told him.

"Is that an invitation?"

"No!" She tried to move away, but there wasn't much room to move.

"Why fight it?" he murmured.

"Fight what?"

"The magic."

She stared at him, trying not to sink into his hypnotist's gaze. "I don't believe in magic," she said.

"No? But it's in you," he answered softly. "There's all kinds of magic. There's the kind that men create, and then there's the special magic one can find only in a woman's eyes..."

Breathless, she gazed up at him, feeling the spell of his seductive, probing gaze radiate through her, as his warm hand slowly slid from the small of her back to her shoulders.

"There's powerful magic in your eyes, Kelly," he whispered.

A sensual shiver pulsed through her as his fingers grazed the back of her neck, playing with the damp tendrils of hair. Ever so slowly, he bent his face to hers. Her upturned face tilted, as if magnetically drawn, to receive his kiss.

His lips were tender, touching and tasting hers as she tasted the brandy lingering in the sweetness of his mouth. His tongue found hers and her lips parted wider.

Then he pulled her closer to his body, and their kiss melded into a heated, openly erotic union. For a sweet, tantalizing, deliciously disorienting moment, she lost herself in the dizzying crush of their embrace. She tasted him with her tongue, and reveled in the answering urgency of his demanding mouth.

But as he shifted his weight to lean back, bringing her pliant body lined against his own, Kelly resisted, her sudden excitement turning to a flush of fear. What in the world was she doing?

Her eyes flicked open and she gently but firmly pushed

her palms against his chest, backing away from him, her head spinning and her heart pounding.

"This is a bad idea," she said, breathing heavily.

He shook his head. "It's the best."

"Look," she began weakly.

"I can't stop looking," he said in a husky low voice.

"That's the problem," she muttered, forcing herself to break the spell that was binding her to his eyes by moving away. She glanced downward to make sure she wasn't about to fall down the steps.

"Why not stay?" he asked softly.

She shook her head and, looking at him again, focused on his eyebrows to avoid his hypnotic eyes. "I've stayed too long already," she said. "I have to go home."

"Is someone waiting for you?"

Kelly cleared her throat. "No."

"Then..."

"Look," she said, "if you're serious about entering into a professional relationship with me—with *Omnibus*—I think we'd both be best off putting an end to this kind of thing right now."

"What kind of thing do you see it as?" he asked, stroking the end of his mustache, his hand hiding the beginnings of a grin.

"Nothing. Except you're pretty good with those deep brown eyes of yours and you know it, Mister Conjurer," she said dryly.

"You're no slouch yourself, Miss Robbins."

"Wait a minute. Are you trying to say—that I—?" she began, indignant, then stopped, glowering at the innocent pose he'd assumed. "I'm leaving," she finished abruptly. "How do you open the door to this thing?"

"Are you going to talk to your editor?"

Kelly glared at him. "Yes."

"First thing in the morning?"

She sighed. "I will." The cat was rubbing against her leg. She grabbed it.

"Wonderful. I really appreciate it," he said earnestly, and, leaning over, he pulled the silver knob protruding from a crank by the driver's seat. The door to the trailer swung open with a hydraulic hiss behind her.

"Thanks for your... assistance," she said, turning to go.

"It was more than a pleasure," was his amused reply.

Kelly walked down the carpeted steps and quickly strode across the pavement to her building in the drizzle, not looking back. A few hard raps on Heidi's window got the woman's attention. Once inside the building, she was divested of the cat by Heidi's grateful next-door neighbor.

Soon Kelly was trudging up the three flights to her apartment, her blood starting to simmer. What nerve, his suggesting *she'd* been the one with the seductive come-on in her eyes! As if *he* hadn't been making eyes at her from the moment they'd met. As if she was attracted to him, as if she'd wanted him to kiss her, to take her in his arms...

She paused at the walk-up's first landing. Let's face it, she told herself. You did want him to. And you enjoyed it.

With a shiver, Kelly walked on. What a fearful prospect—after having only recently recovered from the most devastating relationship in her life—more of the same? She'd thrown herself into her work, and it had paid off in spades: being single, with a singleminded devotion to her career. The last thing she wanted was an involvement with some devious, shady illusionist who was already jeopardizing her reputation with his passion for exposé...

Maybe the whole thing would blow right over. Maybe Albert would think further coverage of Wolfgang Lang or parapsychology was a big waste of magazine space. Sure, he'd resisted her article in the first place! He was bound to hate the idea.

"I love it!" crowed Albert delightedly, leaning back in his chair. "This guy is tremendous!"

Kelly bit her lip and glanced quickly around the conference room. Bruce Perlstein, the senior editor who specialized in science articles, was leaning across the table, his slack-jawed gaze a caricature of astonishment. Cynthia Bullens, associate editor of popular culture, was shaking her head in wonderment. And the managing editor, Peter Gries,

Under His Spell

who usually stopped talking only when forcibly silenced, was mutely staring at the man on the other side of the table.

Julian Sharpe had just read Peter's mind.

Peter had drawn a picture on a pad, making sure to keep the sheet of paper hidden from the magician's view. After a moment's concentration, Julian had drawn a picture on his own pad that was a remarkable facsimile of Peter's. And he had done the same with both Cynthia and Bruce before that. This was a feat that had made Wolfgang Lang famous.

Julian had arrived, sans Siegfried, late in the afternoon the following day, after Kelly informed him she'd been able to set up a meeting. Albert had given her a hard time at first, grumbling about reschedulings and backed-up deadlines, but a perverse desire to see Kelly in an awkward position had won out.

Now he was beaming, tapping the edge of his pipe against the conference table. "Mr. Sharpe," he said, "would you be willing to explain to us the method you use? I appreciate your adeptness at bamboozlement, but I would like to know just how I've been bamboozled."

Julian glanced at Kelly, then looked back at the balding editor. "At the moment, I'd rather not reveal my method. If you decide to give our article the go-ahead..." He held his palms up.

"All right, all right," Albert muttered. He relit his pipe, nodding, and furrowed his brow. Kelly was familiar with this practiced brow furrowing. It indicated he was stalling, thinking of matters more financial than journalistic. Albert hated sanctioning articles with large built-in travel expenses. "So the Halliford Institute's in San Diego," he mused. "What other stops?"

"There's a psychic conference in Chicago and a major parapsychology convention in Colorado," said Julian. "Both worth covering."

"Need a photographer," Albert muttered, his brow's furrows deepening.

"Well, there's still some over-matter from the... other article," Kelly said carefully. "Halliford won't allow photos, I'm sure. But of course, it might be good to get some coverage of the Sharpe Brothers..."

She could feel Julian's eyes upon her. He was trying to understand why she was taking this tack. But she had a card up her own sleeve, and now that Albert was convinced the story was worth doing, she had to play it. "You know who would really be good for this?" she said suddenly, as if the idea had just occurred to her. "Norman Ross." She avoided looking at Julian.

Bruce nodded assent. Cynthia murmured an appreciative agreement. Peter pursed his lips. "You're right," he said. "He's the only one we've got who's as good a photographer as he is a journalist."

"And he did a fantastic job on those Indian mystics," Kelly reminded him. "He's a natural to do this story—and you cut corners on costs." She turned expectantly to Albert. But Albert was shaking his head.

"Nope," he said, and he chomped down on his pipe.

"But—" Kelly began, her heart sinking.

"No way." Albert leaned one elbow on the long table and pointed his pipe at Kelly. "Listen, Robbins, it's bad enough that you got taken in by this—magician in psychic's clothing, and we went ahead and printed it. If you think you're going to wriggle out of your responsibility in this mess, forget it! You started it, you finish it. You're going on the road, gal!"

Coloring, Kelly stared back at her boss. Out of the corner of her eye, she sensed a subtle smirk on Julian Sharpe's face.

"Then you'll do the story?" he asked Albert.

Albert squinted at the ceiling. "It's a lot of airfare," he mused aloud. "With stopovers, hotels..."

"Oh, you don't have to worry about that," Julian said. "I've got a trailer with sleeping accommodations. I was planning to take it westward anyway. We can do the whole trip by highway, if you'll put up the gas."

"But—" Kelly sat up, horrified. "I can't—"

"That's perfect!" Albert told the magician. "We'll do it. I buy the premise, and I'll buy the piece. You've read our minds, you've bent a key—and you're a total shyster!" he exclaimed, shaking his head.

Under His Spell

Kelly ground her teeth, glaring at Julian. She could think of a few other choice words with which to describe him.

"And I certainly wouldn't mind *Omnibus* being the first magazine," Albert went on, "to blow the whistle on that ...that..." He was feeling in his breast pocket, frowning.

"You left your tobacco on your desk," Julian said. "But if you look in Ms. Bullens' jacket, I think you'll find some."

Startled, Albert turned to Cynthia. "Nonsense," she said, with an annoyed glance at Julian. "I don't have—"

"Left pocket," Julian suggested amiably.

Cynthia looked at him. Then, with a shrug, she reached into her pocket—and produced Albert's pouch of Durham tobacco. "I haven't the faintest." She smiled, embarrassed, as Albert took it from her.

"Levitation," Julian said gravely.

There was a moment's shocked silence in the room. Then everybody present began to laugh. Except for one.

"I suppose you're proud of yourself," Kelly grumbled, as she and Julian walked down the corridor to her office.

"I am," Julian admitted. "I can't wait to get started."

"Don't you have tours to do? I thought you and your brother were busy men."

"We always take the summer off," Julian said, suavely ushering her into her own office. "We like to work out new routines, at the farm."

"Right, the farm..." She indicated a chair for him to sit in and went around her desk. "What do you raise there, rabbits? To pull from hats?"

"Cows," he said, stretching out his legs.

She sat. "You pull cows out of hats?"

"Kelly, I hate to disillusion you, but we don't pull anything from hats. We make Siegfried disappear and reappear in a basket, but as far as hats go..."

"Old hat," she suggested.

"That's right." He smiled at her, straightened up, and leaned forward, his eyes twinkling. "If you're really nice, maybe we'll teach you how to appear in a basket, too."

"No, thanks," she said grimly. "I was perfectly happy appearing regularly behind this desk. Then you had to come along, you and your leopard and your bright ideas..." She glared at him, still simmering over Julian's suave maneuvering to get her as a travel companion. "I feel like I'm being kidnapped," she snapped. Then, with a sigh, as Julian merely smiled, she consulted her datebook. "When's Lang due in Chicago?"

"Saturday. That should give us plenty of time."

"For what?"

He looked at her, mustache twitching mischievously. "To prepare for our trip. Orientation—training—research—dinner."

"Dinner?"

"Thanks, I'd love to." He grinned. "It's on *Omnibus*, I assume?"

Kelly shot him a look. "I'm busy tonight."

"Tomorrow night, then," he pronounced airily. "The day after that, we've got to get moving." He rose, obviously considering the matter settled. "I'll pick you up at six. In the meantime..." Julian reached over and lifted the crystal paperweight from her desktop. Beneath it was a piece of black paper with silver writing on it. "There's a booklist for you."

Warily, Kelly lifted the paper and scanned the titles. *"Dark Dimensions—Astral Traveling.* Where do I find these? Hail the next UFO I sight?"

"Try Wyler's, downtown—it specializes in the occult and such."

"Well, I've got a library card, if you haven't palmed it," she said.

"Kelly," Julian said softly, leaning over the desk. She avoided his eyes. "We're going to have a wonderful time."

"You're awfully sure of yourself," she replied, staring at his tanned hands on the desktop. "Next you'll be telling me the vibrations are speaking to you, or something."

"They are," he chuckled. "You'll see."

His hands left the desk. She took a last look at the black paper and tucked it in her datebook. When she looked up, Julian Sharpe was out the door. All that was missing was a puff of smoke.

Chapter 3

THE SUN AND KELLY were barely up when she descended the front steps of her building two days later, a traveling bag in each hand. The door to Julian's gleaming trailer was open, but she had a little difficulty navigating the first step up. One of the two bags, weighted with the heavy tomes she'd bought (and had yet to read) at Julian's request, threw her off balance.

"Here, I'll take those."

Kelly looked up. Julian, attired in tight black jeans and shirt, stood a few steps up, his arms outstretched for her bags. Kelly thought she could detect an expression of typically chauvinistic condescension on his smiling face. Determined to show him she needed no assistance, she managed to sidle through the doorway with the bags, ignoring his offer.

She wobbled uncertainly on the second step, but with an effort that she made great pains to conceal, she ascended the steps, nearly colliding with Julian as she reached the top. Once more, he reached for her bags.

"I'll just put these in the back."

"No, I can handle them."

They were now engaged in a mini tug-of-war for possession of her bags. Julian took hold of her wrists. As she pulled them back, she suddenly found herself pressed up against him. A mixture of shock and unwelcome arousal coursed through her as she felt the warm, firm contours of his chest impress her softer curves. Julian was looking down at her, his eyes gleaming with sensual invitation.

"Well, good morning," he murmured, bringing his face to meet hers.

Kelly did the only sane thing she could think of. She dropped her bags. With a grimace of pain, Julian let go.

"Good morning," she said brightly.

"I'll just take these," he muttered ruefully, lifting one of them off his foot.

"Where are you taking them?" she countered.

"To the back." He was starting down the aisle.

"Wait a second," she said. But Julian continued onward, carrying the bags toward what she knew was his bedroom. "Hold it!" she called. Julian was still walking. Kelly brought her fingers to her lips and let out an ear-splitting whistle.

Julian froze and dropped the bags with a quiet thud. Then he turned, looking at her with amused admiration. "Powerful lungs," he commented.

Slowly, Kelly sauntered down the aisle to meet him halfway, her hands on her hips. When they were a yard from each other, she stopped and leaned back against the counter, her arms folded. "Now, listen," she said, and cleared her throat.

"I'm all ears," he said, and folded his arms as well.

All eyes was more like it, she noted silently. Though she had purposefully dressed down, in an oversized man-tailored shirt, comfortably baggy beige pants wrapped at the waist with a belt and scarf, one simple brass bracelet and small earrings, and minimal makeup, he was still looking at her with an openly sensual gleam in his eye, as if, she registered with a shiver, she was wearing nothing at all.

Kelly tried to keep her own expression cool. She was determined that things shouldn't get any further out of hand than they already were. That he seemed bent on seducing her was bad enough—worse was her fearful apprehension that ultimately, she might not be strong enough to resist him...

"Let's just make one thing crystal clear," she said evenly. "You and I have entered into what's known as a professional relationship. That's the *only* kind of relationship I'm interested in on this trip. Regardless of your assumptions—"

Julian opened his mouth to protest, but she barreled on, ignoring him.

"—I have no intention of sharing that bedroom with you, let alone the bed itself. No offense intended," she added. "I'm sure you've provided wonderful accommodations for... a great number of—guests," she went on, narrowing her eyes as he began to smile, stroking his mustache. "But I'm just not interested, okay? This is business. Now, don't give me *that* look," she continued, as his smile was replaced with an expression of affronted innocence. "I've been around the block. The only major difference between a traveling magician and a traveling musician is a few letters of the alphabet. I've got a pretty good idea what an entertainer's life on the road is like. Me, I'm a journalist, and this—is a job," she finished, and took a breath. "Okay?" she finished hesitantly.

Julian nodded slowly. "Are you done?"

"I am," she said.

"I like a woman who speaks her mind," he said congenially. "Not that it was necessary, though—I've been planning to sleep on the couch here. The room in the back is all yours."

Kelly felt her cheeks start to burn under his insouciant gaze.

"I already changed the sheets for you," he was saying, "and I was just going to stow these bags back there. But if you'd rather keep them up front—"

"That's okay," she said a little stiffly.

"They'll keep where they are for now, I guess," he said. Then he gestured toward the front of the bus with a mockly formal, expansive sweep of his arm. "Shall we hit the road? I mean, now that we know where we stand?"

Blushing, she imagined, from the roots of her hair to the toes of her sandals, Kelly preceded Julian up the aisle. The snake, her mind muttered angrily, he'd really enjoyed that little exchange. Well, she'd set herself up, hadn't she? With his help...

Her seat was separated from Julian's by two feet of aisle space. She settled into the comfortable leather upholstery, ignoring what she assumed was his smirking expression. The hydraulic hiss of the bus door shutting synchronized with the gunning rumble of the motor, and they were off.

"Here's our map," he said, handing it to her. "You're the navigator."

"Okay." She perused it. "George Washington Bridge?"

"You got it."

The early morning vista of the relatively deserted Upper East Side glimmered in the huge, oversized windshield. They were higher above the road than she was used to being, and it felt odd to be there, instead of getting ready for work with the rest of the city. So long, serenity, she thought silently, finding it ironic that the imminent metropolitan hustle and bustle should suddenly seem safe and placid compared to this odyssey ahead of her.

She stole a look at Julian. Relaxed, in his element, he sat back in the driver's seat with only one hand on the wheel. Strong profile, she observed, as the first shaft of direct sunlight illuminated his face. The way his hair casually, though rakishly, swept back from his forehead—

Kelly looked away, concentrating on the map again, and cleared her throat. What was that line about the lady protesting too much? It seemed she was going to have trouble keeping her mind on business even without his pursuit... She stifled a sigh, and stared at the map. "Are we driving straight through?"

"Well, I'd like to stop around noon and take Sig for a walk while we grab some lunch."

She'd almost forgotten they had a leopard for cargo. Briefly, she wondered what a cat that size ate for lunch, but decided she didn't want to know. She checked her watch. "Maybe midway through Pennsylvania?"

Julian nodded. "And dinner when we hit the Indiana border."

"That looks right," she agreed, and folded the map.

"So," said Julian. "Did you get all your homework done? The work that precluded our dinner date?"

Kelly had wriggled out of dinner with him the night before under the pretense of doing some research, though she'd done it more as a concerted effort to keep her distance. "Uh-huh," she said. "I was busy all night."

Under His Spell   47

"Where?" he asked casually, as they turned onto the entrance to the bridge. "You weren't home or at the office."

So he'd called. For some reason that both pleased and annoyed her. "I was...out," she told him.

"What's he like?" Julian went on. "Short like you or tall like me?"

"Neither," Kelly sighed. "I wasn't out with a man." Actually, she'd had dinner with Bruce Perlstein, who was going to do some research on Wolfgang and magicians for her while she was gone. Though she liked the affable staff member, it was certainly a purely platonic relationship.

"That's surprising," Julian said. "You're not my idea of a spinster."

Unwittingly, she rose to the bait. "Don't you think there's a middle ground between spinsterhood and...promiscuity?" she asked defensively. "Just because I wasn't on a date last night—" She stopped abruptly, realizing her mistake. She wasn't about to get involved in a conversation this personal.

But Julian, of course, had no qualms. "I suppose there is," he said breezily. "How many men do you usually date, on the average? That is, if you date more than one. Do you?"

"I'm sure I couldn't keep up with your current tally," she said wryly. "But this conversation isn't my idea of a good way to begin our professional relationship. Do you think we could stick to—"

"You seem to have a pretty well-defined image of the kind of man I am," he said, amused. "But for all you know, my preferences, when it comes to women—"

"I'm not interested in your preferences," she snapped, exasperated. "Look, if I'm supposed to be your eyes and ears when I see Wolfgang again, you're going to find yourself deaf and blind. Really, Julian—could we start my crash course in magic? I'd feel more secure if we could."

"All right," he said resignedly. "Why don't you bring that book by Adler up here? I'll point out some relevant passages to you."

"Fine," she said, then went down the aisle to get the book out of her bag. When she returned, they were rolling along the New Jersey Turnpike, a sudden plethora of trees and greenery on all sides. "To tell you the truth," she began tentatively, slipping into her seat, "I haven't had a chance to read—"

"Blondes," Julian announced abruptly.

"What?" she said, startled.

"My preference in women has taken a decided leaning toward blondes." He smiled. "That is, since I met you."

"Sharpe," she said tersely, "stick to business—or I'm off this bus."

Julian pursed his lips, then reflectively stroked his mustache with the back of one thumb. "Okay, lady," he said at length. "We'll play it your way. Read chapters one and two, then skip to five—the section on materializations. Then go back to the library and take out the black folder on famous hoaxes—"

"Library?"

"This is a strictly professional operation," he admonished her gravely. "All reference materials are stored on the shelves on the other side of the door to the bedroom. When you've taken a look at those clippings on hoaxes, I've got a tape for you to listen to of a Milbourne Christopher lecture—"

"Who?"

"He's considered the top magic historian alive. He's written about twenty books, but this lecture distills some of the more relevant things into two hours."

"Two hours?"

Julian shrugged. "We've got plenty of time. Haven't we?"

Kelly looked at him. He'd adopted an archly serious air, concentrating on the road. "I suppose we do," she said.

"That should keep you busy till we hit Pennsylvania," he said. "Say, do me a favor, will you? Pop open that dash compartment and hand me the headphones."

Kelly leaned over, opened the little door, and removed the tiny lightweight phones from the interior. As she handed them to Julian she got a brief glance at the cassettes piled within—an odd melange of classical and country music,

Under His Spell

not the strangest of which was labeled "Johannes Brahms & Johnny Cash." Julian nodded a thanks and plugged the headphones into a tape machine built into the console. He pushed a cassette sticking out of the gate into play position and put on the phones.

"Driving with these on is illegal in some states," he told her. "But let's be bold. I wouldn't want to disturb your concentration. When you're ready for the lecture, they're all yours."

With a friendly smile he settled back in his seat, and soon Kelly could hear, very faintly, the quiet warble of a pedal steel guitar over the motor's vibrant hum. Kelly looked from him to the opened book in her lap.

All right, then. She'd read. Fortunately she wasn't one to get carsick.

Somewhere in Pennsylvania and some indeterminate time later, when her eyes were beginning to cross, Kelly looked up wearily, gladdened to see that they were pulling off the road, into a deserted picnic area by a forest. She cleared her throat. "Lunch?" she croaked, her voice unused to activation after such a long stretch of silence. She and Julian hadn't exchanged a word in hours.

"Uh-huh," he said, turning off the motor. "Why don't you bring those along?"

Rather than interrupt Julian's stoic, mute chauffeuring—two could play at this game of practiced non-communication—Kelly had compiled a list of questions, written on the little pad in her lap. "Okay," she said, and stood up in the aisle after he'd passed, stretching.

She touched her toes with her hands, rubbed the back of her neck, and peered down the aisle. Julian was taking things out of the refrigerator. She sauntered down to get a better look, her stomach grumbling in anticipation, then stopped short—as he plopped a gargantuan raw sirloin wrapped in plastic down on the counter.

"I know I'm hungry," she began. "But isn't that—"

"Siegfried's," he explained. "There's cold cuts for us. Want to make a few sandwiches?"

* * *

She watched the satisfied leopard devour his lunch in record time, from some distance away, as she and Julian strolled through the edge of the forest, sandwiches in hand.

"So it's muscular control," Julian explained, in answer to her question about the art of sleight-of-hand. "The only other disciplines I can think of that require the same kind of rigorous training would be championship gymnastics, or maybe classical piano."

"I see," she said, her eyes involuntarily drawn to Julian's trim and fit physique, musculature vividly outlined by the thin T-shirt he'd changed into before leaving the bus.

"Next question?" he asked, his eyes twinkling as she looked up, embarrassed, to meet his gaze.

"That's as far as I've gotten," she admitted.

"After close-up work comes the larger illusions," he said.

Kelly nodded, then took a deep breath of fresh air, the sun momentarily dazzling her as they emerged from the glade of trees.

"It does smell sweeter, doesn't it?" Julian smiled, then bent to unwrap Siegfried's chain from around the leg of a picnic table. Straightening again, he tilted his head back, drinking the last drops from the carton of milk he'd brought along.

"You always drink milk?" she asked, idly curious.

"When I'm not swilling straight whiskey, as all good traveling entertainers do," he said, with arch sarcasm. "But that's not a professional question, is it?"

"No," she admitted as he grinned.

"Well, you can listen to the Christopher tape next," he mused. "And you can watch the scenery at the same time."

"Great." She sighed.

"Bored so soon?"

"No," she said quickly. "But it is a lot to take in at once."

"It's taken me years," he admitted. "And I'm still learning."

"I can believe that," she said, falling into step beside him. Once again, she was conscious of his looming height, and aware of a strange, intangible sense of security she felt as the rhythm of her steps matched his. Suddenly she sensed him watching her in the silence between them, broken only by the steady jingle of the silver chain clipped to Julian's belt. Siegfried was sauntering through the grass a few yards ahead.

That secure feeling was replaced by a spreading weakness in her legs and knees as he slowed, turning to look at her, the dappled sunlight forming patterns of light and shadow on his tanned and handsome face.

"Hold still," he murmured, and before she could protest, his fingers brushed her cheek in a brief caress. "Dandelion fluff," he said, by way of explanation, but his eyes seemed to glimmer with aroused interest as she trembled involuntarily at his touch. Her cheek was tingling, and she found it hard to break the gaze that passed between them.

"Shouldn't we..." Her voice faltered, sounding unnaturally tremulous to her.

"Be getting back on the road?" he finished for her, a hint of amusement in his tone.

She nodded mutely, feeling abnormally light-headed in the noonday sun. Or was it the concentrated heat of his eyes on hers that made it hard for her to think clearly? Kelly cleared her throat. "Yes," she said. "I've still got a lot of studying to do."

"You sure you don't want to take a longer break?"

There it was again, that soft, insinuatingly sensuous undertone she always sensed in his most innocent remarks. Kelly wondered suddenly if Julian knew quite well the effect he was having on her, despite all her defensive mechanisms. Well, if he was that kind of mind-reader, she'd better short-circuit *his* machinery.

"Of course not," she said breezily, shaking a lock of hair from her eye. "We haven't got all day, right?"

"Right," he agreed, with an insouciant grin. "C'mon, Sig!" A shake of the chain brought the tawny beast bounding to his master's side. Now again a threesome, the travelers boarded the silver bus.

This is going to be difficult, Kelly ruminated, seated once more up front, this time the earphones on her head.

The magic historian's sandpapery voice droned into her ears as the rolling hills and flatlands of Pennsylvania rolled by, but her attention—and all too often, her eyes—kept wandering to the silent man across the aisle. She couldn't help being aware of him, to her increasing frustration. He didn't even have to *do* anything; at the moment he was watching the road, his expression inscrutable, but still she felt his presence. There was something the man radiated, an assured, inner strength that drew her attention to him like a magnet, no matter how hard she concentrated on the history of illusionism.

Kelly leaned forward and stopped the tape briefly, then rewound it. She'd missed at least a full two minutes of the lecture, and hadn't the slightest idea what Christopher was talking about. Stifling a sigh, she leaned back in her seat, closing her eyes to the warmth of the late afternoon sun.

A while later, a soft rippling, crackling sound that had an even cadence made her open her eyes in curiosity. Julian had a card in his left hand. As he drove with his right hand on the wheel, he effortlessly wound the playing card around his fingers, made it appear and disappear, seemingly rolled it between his knuckles, popped it forward, then retracted it—all without looking, or missing a beat. It was obviously an exercise he'd long ago mastered.

Mesmerized, Kelly watched the card move as if alive, a quiet wave of applause signaling the end of the lecture on the tape. Coming to, she took the headphones off. "If you don't mind my asking, Julian—what are...I mean, why are you doing that?"

"Keeping in shape." He leaned to his left briefly, accelerating to pass another vehicle, then settled back, the card still snaking in and around his steadily undulating hand. "Fingers get rusty if I don't keep this up." He glanced at her briefly. "Is it bothering you?"

"No, I was just curious."

"Tape's over?"

Kelly nodded, letting out an involuntary yawn. "Have I completed my course, Professor?"

Julian shook his head. "Not by a long shot. I think you

Under His Spell   53

ought to go back and peruse that Tarbell book on the bottom shelf."

"Really?" She squinted at her wristwatch. "How close are we to dinner?"

"Another couple of hours, if it's all right with you."

Kelly shrugged resignedly. "Where did you get all of this stuff, anyway? A lot of this material is by small presses and such. I didn't think there were extensive magic libraries in Nebraska."

"I've collected books and periodicals from all over the world," he said. "I'm thinking of writing one of my own someday," he added, after a beat.

"Oh?" She turned to look at him more closely, unable to tear her eyes from the card continually rotating around his hand, and the muscles tightening and untightening in his strong forearm. "What on?"

"That's getting a little personal, don't you think?" he said with a mischievous grin. "Time's a-wasting, you know. If you're going to act as my eyes and ears—"

"All right," she said, "I get the message. But I think my brain might get overloaded—"

"Nonsense," he said expansively. "A brilliant mind such as yours? I'm sure you can absorb much, much more . . . And at dinner, we can review. You'll probably have more questions to ask."

Kelly rose, steadying herself against the sway of the trailer's rounding a curve, with a hand on the back of her seat. "Why don't we make dinner a sort of a break?" she suggested tentatively.

Julian raised his eyebrows in mock dismay. "You mean idle chatter? Non-work-related repartee?" He shook his head worriedly.

"You've made your point," she muttered. "I'm glad you find yourself so amusing."

"Merely maintaining professional decorum," he said.

"Right," she said, and left him to his driving and his exercise. The man was insufferable. She didn't want to talk to him, anyway. But as she found the proper book and seated herself on the couch by the kitchen area, the image of his laughing eyes and agile fingers floated across her mind with unnerving clarity...

This trip was seeming longer by the minute.

"Doesn't look like much," Julian murmured as they walked across the little gravel parking lot to the lone diner set off the highway. "But I bet the food's good. Truck route, you know."

"I could eat almost anything," said Kelly. "This place is fine with me."

Dusk was settling in a musky rust glow over fenced pastures dotted with the figures of distant cows, beyond the long, ramshackle building. It resembled one of those pre-World War II Depression diners she'd seen in Walker Evans' photos of the Dust Bowl, Kelly decided, as Julian held open the creaking screen door for her. The interior was clean and quaint, with a black-and-white-checker-tiled floor and chromium stools along the counter, and faded Coca-Cola posters from the fifties still stuck above the grill. The latter would fetch a pretty penny in a New York City antiques shop, she reflected, as they eased into a booth in the corner.

"Something smells good," Julian commented, lowering his shoulderbag onto the seat beside him, "though the atmosphere could use a little sprucing up..." He unfolded his napkin, shook it once, and when he dropped it, there was a bouquet of colorful flowers in his hand.

Kelly gasped, startled.

"For you." Julian smiled, handing her the bouquet, which, on closer inspection, turned out to be made of paper. "You don't have to put them in water," he joked.

"Well, I—thank you," she said, and made a show of sniffing their imaginary scent. She propped them up between the ashtray and mustard bottle by the wall. "Yes, that does make a difference," she admitted, with a smile.

"Let's see..." His eyes were drawn to the yellow-shaded light on the wall above the table. A glance to the counter assured him their waitress wasn't yet en route. Julian reached up, deftly unscrewed the light bulb, and waved his hand with a flourish over the table—producing, with his other

Under His Spell

hand, when it emerged from below, a small lit candle in a glass holder.

Kelly laughed, shaking her head. "You're an incorrigible romantic, I see."

Julian shrugged, placing the candle near the flowers. "I just can't resist a fresh audience. But this is an improvement, isn't it?"

With the colorful bouquet and the flickering soft candlelight, their little corner of the diner did indeed have a romantic glow all its own. Julian had transformed the cozy but worn-down booth with these simple and seductive touches into something faintly...magical. "Yes," she admitted, meeting his gaze. "You've improved it."

Julian shook his head. "I'm only setting the scene for you, Kelly," he said softly. "Any ordinary place you sit becomes...extraordinary."

The velvet depths of his soft dark eyes glimmered in the candlelight, caressing her features. Feeling a tremor of aroused response as his glistening gaze seemed to drink in her face, Kelly forced herself to break the spell. "I'm sure you say that to all the girls," she joked.

The softness in Julian's expression disappeared, replaced by a harder, opaque look. "Just to some," he said gruffly, and he turned his eyes to the pad on the table by her place setting. "Okay, Miss Omnibus—let's get back to work."

After the waitress, unfazed by Julian's mood lighting, took their orders, the magician kept the conversation all business. Kelly felt a twinge of regret that she'd been so defensive. After a long day of mundane exchanges, she actually would have enjoyed some low-key flirtation. Just as well, she told herself, and she concentrated on her notes and the food, which was simply prepared but delicious.

"Misdirection?" Julian chewed thoughtfully on his chicken wing, then put it down. "Well, you plot out your trick so that the weakest point is minimized by misleading talk, or action. Say I'm going to perform some trickery with your French fries," he went on. "I might talk about their origins. Did you know these fries were probably cut from the local fields' harvest?" He gestured at the window, and Kelly's eyes were involuntarily drawn to the darkening vista outside. "Where's your last fry?"

It was no longer on her plate.

"It's in your other hand, mister," said their waitress, who had reappeared in the aisle at Kelly's side, her hands on her hips.

Julian looked up at her with a smile. "So it is," he agreed, and popped the potato strip into his mouth.

"Just don't try any of that funny stuff when it comes to payin' the check," the matronly woman grumbled good-naturedly. "Coffee?"

Kelly nodded, and Julian, too. The woman trundled off to get them cups. Kelly studied Julian thoughtfully as he finished his last bite of chicken. "I noticed one thing in my reading," she said. "Most magicians start out when they're children. None of them seems to have taken it up as an adult. Is that true for you?"

Julian nodded. "My mother gave me a little set of magic tricks when I was six. Fascinated me." He turned toward the window, thinking back. "I mastered the bunch and started inventing my own. The thing that amazed me was the mechanics involved—all it took was the know-how and some physical discipline, and you could make the impossible come true..." He paused, smiling to himself. "One time, a cup-and-ball rig that I invented disappeared in the wink of an eye, though, and it scared me out of my wits."

"What do you mean?" she asked. "How? Real magic?"

Julian chuckled. "No, my brother stole it. He was working on a few scams of his own."

"He'd been learning from you?"

Julian nodded. "But if you ask him, he'll say it was the other way around. At any rate, we teamed up. We had a lot of time on our hands," he added, with a rueful chuckle. "You grew up in a small town, Kelly. You know how it is."

Kelly nodded. The long stretches of time with little to do glimmered faintly in her memory. She remembered endless afternoons, off by herself when her older brothers were busy being boys... and then the shock of the big city, like

Under His Spell

falling through ice in a pond. And the struggle to stay above the surface in the churning depths of the city—

"What are you thinking about?" he asked softly. "You look sad."

"Really?" She shook off the thoughts, forcing a smile. "I was just mulling over what you said. Smalltown life does move slowly. I had a lot of time on my hands, too. I guess I had my own sort of games."

"A fantasy world?" He smiled. "That was the fun of doing magic. You could make fantasies real."

"In a way. I dreamed of being a famous writer. Like... Willa Cather. A pioneer poetess..." She smiled, embarrassed. "Whenever I was alone, I'd make up stories, write imaginary poems. Words were like playmates."

"Didn't you come from a big family?"

"All men," she said shortly. "I was already the odd girl out, and then—well, my mom died when I was eight, and we moved..." She stopped uncertainly. She hadn't meant to stir up those murky old feelings. She was always afraid if she let them loose, they'd overwhelm her.

"It must have been tough for you," Julian said softly, and his warm hand closed over hers on the Formica tabletop. "We lost both our folks when I was just out of my teens," he added. "It's a painful thing—to say the least."

She wanted to pull her hand away. But his touch felt good. Her hand felt warm and secure in his, and for a long, quiet moment she just sat there very still, looking at his slender fingers clasped over hers. She realized, dimly shocked, that she didn't really want to move her hand, and that a warmth was spreading from his palm to her hand and arm and chest and lower... Kelly looked up. His eyes were softly glowing, his lips pursed slightly in a seductively inviting way—

The plunk of china cups on the table broke the silence. Suddenly self-conscious, Kelly removed her hand as the waitress moved away again. She glanced behind her. But other than an old man in faded workclothes sipping coffee at the counter, she and Julian were the sole residents of this homey little diner off the turnpike in Ohio. Nonetheless, she put her hand demurely in her lap, as if removing it from view would erase the sensations she'd been starting to feel when Julian touched her.

See what happens when the conversation veers from professional to personal matters? Kelly took a sip of coffee, silently reminding herself that the moment of fleeting kinship she'd felt with her companion shouldn't sway her. What kind of kinship could she really have with a man who was as unmoored and unattached to anyone or anything as that silver trailer that gleamed dully under a sole streetlamp outside the diner?

"When's your next tour start?" she asked abruptly, avoiding Julian's questioning gaze.

He paused, then drummed his fingers on the tabletop in a tacit reminder that a moment ago her hand had been there, and they'd been talking of other things. Then, with a tone of resignation, he told her, "Supposed to be September. Jimmy wants to take the show up north for a change. Canada, or maybe even Europe."

Maybe Europe. The phrase had a familiar ring. Kelly looked at the magician directly now, narrowing her eyes until she could almost see Richard sitting there. That's what he'd always said: Europe on the next tour, Europe sounded good. And you and me? We'll work it out...

"Did I say something wrong?"

Kelly sighed, and looked away again. "No, I'm sorry," she said, "My mind's wandering. I think a full day of travel and study's starting to take its toll on me."

"I'll bet," he said sympathetically. "We should move on. There's a trailer park over the Indiana border where I figured we could camp for the night. Should be just another hour or so of driving."

"Sounds good to me," Kelly told him.

"Will there be anything else?"

Julian looked up at the waitress. "Well, not unless you've got about ten pounds of raw meat you can spare, Miss—a little something for my friend out in the bus."

The waitress fixed Julian with an incredulous stare.

Under His Spell

"Who's your friend? The Werewolf of London?"

Julian smiled. "Lady, you'd never believe me."

"Everything okay in there?"

Kelly froze in the act of putting toothbrush to teeth. She had been in the little bathroom of the trailer for a long time, she realized—mainly because she dreaded appearing in her pajamas and robe in front of Julian, and so she'd dawdled over every act of readying herself for sleep.

"Fine," she called, over the steady stream of water from the sink faucet. "I'll be out in a second."

She brushed her teeth vigorously, once, twice—gargled with warm water long beyond the call of duty—but soon could think of no other invention to keep her inside. Face scrubbed, teeth clean to the point of aching gums, she emerged at last.

Julian was seated casually on his couch, attired in the maroon robe she'd worn on her first visit—and nothing else, she noted immediately with a quiver of excited apprehension. Well, what had she expected? It was a warm night, and she was the one almost ludicrously overdressed.

"Wine?" He was offering her a glass. "A little nightcap."

"No, thanks," she said quickly, remembering what brandy and soft maroon robes had brought on in her last visit.

"You don't mind if I do, I hope."

"No, of course not."

She stood awkwardly by the bathroom, as if ready to retreat, her eyes deviously drawn to the open collar of his robe, where a sexy tangle of dark chest hair was all too visible on his tanned skin. His long, muscular bare legs were stretched out before him.

Kelly felt her heart beating faster in her chest as she drew her own robe instinctively tighter. She sensed him shrewdly appraising her as he sipped his wine. Good Lord, was he going to sit here like this all night? Or would he have the decency to—

"Well," he said abruptly, swinging his legs down and rising with a lithe animal-like grace. "You've got clean sheets, pillowcases... I don't know as you'll need the blanket, what with all that you've got on."

She ignored his somewhat insolent smile, looking dumbly at the bed. "Thanks," she said, not knowing what else to say.

"You know, there's something about you in a robe," he said thoughtfully, stepping toward her. She took a step back. "It gives me... thoughts."

"Keep them to yourself," she suggested, with a smile. "Well! I'm beat. Guess I'll turn in."

He smiled back, clearly enjoying her obvious nervousness. There was a rustle from the black tarp opposite the bed, and Kelly unthinkingly took a step in the other direction, bringing her right into Julian's arms.

"Change your mind?" he said huskily, holding her gently by the elbows, a sensuous gleam in his velvet dark eyes.

"I—no, it's—" She stepped away, gesturing toward the tarp, and the unseen animal behind it.

"Oh," he said, smiling. "Don't worry about Sig. He's chained and caged. Besides, he's a sound sleeper. Unless you're a loud snorer."

"I'm not," she said indignantly, feeling a flush creep into her cheeks. A chill had gone up her spine when he'd briefly held her, and the goosebumps hadn't gone down yet. "Well, good night."

"Good night," he said, with studied casualness, his eyes seeming to drink her in from head to foot before he turned away. "Sweet dreams," he called over his shoulder, and then pulled the doors shut behind him with a gentlemanly bow.

Alone in the room Kelly quickly doused the lights and slipped beneath the bedcovers. Once she felt safe enough, she quietly removed her robe and unbuttoned her pajama top a bit, as it was warm enough, actually, to...

Sleep in the nude? As she did at home? No way; not in a million years. It wasn't that she couldn't trust him. She sensed that he'd been flirting more to tease her than anything else and he was certainly too much of a gentleman to try...

Through the crack in the doors she saw the lights in the

other room go out, and heard the rustle of Julian's body settling down on the couch. She was suddenly vividly aware that his body—naked or near naked—was reclining only a few yards away, and this awareness sent a prickly chill of deliciously wicked arousal through her own body.

You idiot, she told herself, what's the matter with you? Count sheep, count playing cards... With a quiet moan, she turned her face into the pillow. An answering little yawn reached her from behind the tarp and she stiffened again in the darkness.

She didn't know which made her more nervous—the man or the beast. But between the two of them, she didn't expect to sleep a wink.

Chapter 4

BOYCE HALL WAS an imposing, tall modernistic building in downtown Chicago. As she walked up the steps she scanned the milling groups of people, wondering if Julian was among them. He'd dropped her off an hour earlier, many blocks from the site of the conference, taking no chances that Wolfgang Lang or any of his associates would sight the Sharpe Brothers' silver bus in the vicinity. Not paranoia, he assured her, but precaution—and furthermore, he'd join her in the auditorium— in disguise—where Lang was scheduled to speak.

"You won't recognize me," he said. "But I'll find you. Leave the seat next to you empty for me."

"This is a little much," Kelly said. "What makes you think—"

"I've already gone on record saying Lang's a fake," Julian said. "You, on the other hand, are a true believer. I don't want anybody putting the two of us together."

Kelly had shrugged, figuring Julian knew what he was doing. Now she wended her way through a maze of halls, flashing her press card at the officious-looking people who stopped her en route to the main auditorium's dressing room. Her mission was to gain entrance into the inner sanctum.

This was made easier than she'd thought when she encountered Fritz Murnau just outside it. The prematurely balding, flashily attired, and perennially beaming companion of Wolfgang's was extremely happy to see her. He graciously led her to the room where the psychic stood surrounded by a small cluster of admirers. Kelly noted that Wolfgang was getting the royal treatment; a buffet of cold cuts and pâtés had been laid out against the mirrored counter,

Under His Spell

with red and white wine on tap, as well as a number of harried-looking Boyce Hall staff members, who were quick to respond to any of their guests' requests.

"Ah, Miss Robin!" Wolfgang Lang approached her, hand outstretched, a dazzling smile on his angular face, his hawk-like nose reddened with a newly acquired sunburn. Kelly smiled back, shaking the man's hand. He held hers much longer than mere politeness required. "I expect you!" Wolfgang exclaimed. "I knew that you... come back to me!"

Startled, Kelly stared at the long-haired psychic. She hadn't phoned Fritz before coming. For a moment, she had the horrified feeling that Wolfgang somehow knew what she was up to. He was chuckling now at her expression, and, turning to Fritz, said a few words in German.

"He felt your presence," Fritz explained to her with a smug smile. "Wolfgang knew that the two of you would meet again."

"Your magazine..." Wolfgang narrowed his eyes at her, his bushy black eyebrows meeting as he melodramatically concentrated. "It sells... more—great success, because of Wolfgang, I am right? You come—for more of me! You want more interview."

Kelly nodded, recovering her composure. As she launched into her prepared pitch, she mused that, if not psychic, Wolfgang was certainly glowing with the energy of pure egotism. The two Germans swallowed her bait avariciously. Fritz consented to a follow-up piece without a moment's hesitation, and he presented her with an itinerary of their tour, entering her name on their official guest-pass list. Wolfgang's interest in her was more than professional, she noted, but she supposed that was all to the good. She hung on his every utterance with rapt attention, masking the discomfort she felt at his pursuit.

"If you have some time after the... ah, lecture," she began.

"Of course, you cannot have enough of me." He smiled. "And more—amazing things I have to tell you," he informed her eagerly. "I make miracles!"

Kelly tried to show awed amazement. Then she, along

with other visitors, was ushered from the backstage area. Wolfgang needed to "clear his aura" before going on, according to Fritz, who stuffed a backstage pass into her hand as he shooed press members from the room.

Mission accomplished, Kelly made her way to the auditorium and found a seat fairly close to the front, making sure to keep the aisle seat next to her empty. As she waited for the lights to dim, she looked around her, taking mental notes on the character of the audience. Other than a man in a turban and a couple in matching tie-dyed purple jumpsuits, on the whole the people who'd come to see Wolfgang Lang looked like... people, she decided. Markedly normal in appearance and demeanor, the crowd could have been attending a movie or a concert.

But hadn't she, after all, been taken in just as these people had, or were about to be? Fidgeting in her seat with a mixture of embarrassment and impatience, Kelly compared her first impressions of Wolfgang with her view of him now. Armed with the knowledge she'd gained from Julian, the so-called psychic's pomposity and melodramatic pontifications seemed transparently absurd to her now. And his successful flim-flamming of America seemed to have made him all the more obnoxiously cocky.

Then there was Julian. Funny, but the magician's air of calm pragmatism seemed the antithesis of crackpot occultism to her, and his single-minded pursuit of Wolfgang was making more sense. Lang, with his bogus "aura" and miracle-making, would have been perfectly in his element alongside the historic charlatans she'd been reading up on— colorful quacks with show-biz flair. But these people around her had paid money to see "the real thing." Julian's brief tutelage was already endowing her with a sense of indignation at the hucksterism Wolfgang embodied.

Where was Julian? Had he encountered trouble getting in? Kelly glanced worriedly down the aisle. She realized, with a little flush of embarrassment, that in the short time they'd been traveling together, she'd already grown accustomed to having him constantly at her side. It felt odd to be suddenly alone again.

Under His Spell

Her thoughts slipped back to last night, when she'd slept fitfully, all too aware that she wasn't alone. In the morning, she'd woken to find Julian up and making breakfast. When she got dressed—in a summery white linen dress with a lot of bare shoulder, high heels, and more accentuated makeup—she was a little confused as to whether she was dressing up for Wolfgang Lang or the man scrambling eggs on the other side of the partition. Julian had greeted her appearance with a raised eyebrow and a low whistle, which she shamelessly enjoyed, though she affected a demeanor of annoyance. It was becoming harder not to show that she appreciated being appreciated. Julian's attractiveness seemed to increase the more she got to know him; a most unfortunate development...

The lights were dimming. Kelly nervously checked the aisle. An elderly white-haired and bearded man with a cane paused at her side and began to lower himself into the empty seat. "Excuse me," Kelly whispered apprehensively. "But this seat's taken."

"It certainly is." The man wheezed, seated now and not budging.

"Sir," Kelly began, annoyed, "I'm sorry, but—"

"Give me any more heat and I'll sic a leopard on ya," the man whispered. "Or I'll hide your pajamas."

Kelly's jaw dropped. "Julian?" she whispered.

He rapped her foot with his cane. "Professor Hilliard to you, young lady," he hissed. "Let's watch the show."

Kelly couldn't suppress a grin of amused respect at Julian's skills with makeup. Even at this close range, he looked to be at least sixty. In the darkness, he patted her hand in a fatherly fashion, only the markedly youthful twinkle in his eye giving him away.

"Here he comes," Julian whispered. "Now remember, when I nudge you, don't watch what Lang is directing you to watch. Keep your eye on him, or on his friend Murnau there..."

A cresting wave of applause drowned out his next words. The famous psychic and his companion were entering the spotlight.

* * *

Kelly scanned the crowd at the bar of Charley's, the restaurant in the downtown area where Julian had said he'd meet her. She wasn't sure whether to expect a white-haired or black-haired Julian. The white-haired version had slipped away at the end of Wolfgang's performance, leaving her to go backstage and socialize with the psychic some more.

"Over here!"

It was Julian the younger. He was motioning her over to a table on the other side of the softly lit, smoky room. Kelly made her way through the well-dressed throng of people who seemed mostly young, and in animatedly high spirits. Julian had mentioned that Charley's catered to people in the entertainment world of Chicago, and she recognized the atmosphere and tone of the place as being similar to such clubs in the east. She'd frequented them with Richard, "in" watering holes where the talk was witty and flowed as fast as the liquor.

As she approached Julian's table, Kelly slowed her stride. Julian, dressed in his characteristic black, was being kissed on the cheek by a tall, svelte blonde in a fashionable, diaphanous dress. She seemed to be an old—and possibly intimate—acquaintance, from the look of their affectionate exchange. But she was gone by the time Kelly took her seat.

"Friend of yours?" Kelly asked him, watching the receding low-cut back of the woman's dress. A little voice in her head reminded her that she hadn't the least cause for jealousy. She hadn't, of course—she was asking the question only out of polite curiosity.

"That's Lucille Barton," Julian said. "We shared a bill in Vegas a few years back."

Kelly recognized the name of the popular singer. She wondered briefly what else the two entertainers had shared. Stop it, she warned herself. Julian was asking her a question. "Hmm? I'm sorry, Julian, I didn't—"

He smiled. "It is a bit noisy in here, isn't it? But the food's great. I was wondering if you wanted a drink before dinner."

Under His Spell   67

A waiter in suit and tie had appeared, answering Julian's silent summons. "Maybe some wine with dinner," Kelly told Julian. He nodded and got the wine list.

"The seafood's especially good here," he remarked. "So, I assume our Mr. Lang was more than happy to remake your acquaintance."

"Truly," she said, glancing over the menu. "He was exhausted after his demonstration, but he was still willing to talk for a few minutes."

"Naturally." Julian grinned. "The toll must have been great. But when publicity calls..." He shrugged. "Did you take down everything? The things I pointed out?"

Kelly nodded. She'd jotted a few notes in shorthand during Wolfgang's performance, and then had written more extensive descriptions of what she'd seen, after visiting Wolfgang backstage. With Julian's assistance, she'd been able to catch the psychic performing some subtle but unmistakably obfuscating motions as he performed his "feats" before the captive audience. Seated as close to the stage as they were, she'd seen, for example, how the careful alteration of a "blinding" bandage across his eyes had enabled Wolfgang to see more than he was supposed to, while "guessing" what was written on a blackboard across the stage.

She discussed each stage of the "act," as Julian called Wolfgang's demonstration, with Julian as they ate dinner. It was expensive but exquisite food. At Julian's urging, she'd ordered lobster, which was fresh and succulent. She enjoyed every morsel, and the delicious wine he ordered with it. The Sharpe brothers were obviously used to living in style. For all his casual banter and unpretentious dress, she could tell Julian was quite at home in this first-class environment.

"So far, so good," Julian commented, when they'd covered all the relevant points of the conference. "We're getting somewhere, don't you think?"

"Well, thanks to you," she said, unable to ignore the flush of pride she felt at his use of "we." Already she was feeling the pull of duplicity with her partner in what was turning out to be a kind of espionage. She was beginning to feel a new bond with Julian, born of their working together on this "scoop." She liked the feeling.

"When we get to Denver, we'll bring in the hidden camera," Julian mused. "Are you on their guest list now?"

"I'm as in as I can be," Kelly told him, nodding a thanks as he refilled her wineglass. "I haven't directly broached the San Diego issue yet, but I planted seeds. I have a feeling he'll go for it."

"I'm sure he's going for you," Julian said, "in a big way."

Kelly shrugged. "I did a lot of eyelash batting. But it's not even necessary. The man's a complete wolf."

Julian frowned. "Don't let him get too close," he muttered. "I might have to rearrange his sunburned features."

"I can take care of myself," she said.

"Maybe," he said. "But I like taking care of you." He sipped his wine, seeming to savor her with his eyes at the same time. The direct sensuality in his glowing gaze sent a little tremor of excitement down her spine. As he scrutinized her, his eyes traveling slowly from her face to her bare shoulders and her breasts, hugged tightly by the sheer linen, she had the breathless feeling he'd possessively probed her with his hands, and not his eyes.

"I'm just another passenger," she said breezily, trying to keep the mood light. "You don't have to feel any responsibility. I'm sure that's the way you like it."

Julian's eyes narrowed. Then he sat back, with a benign little smile. "Sure," he said easily. Did she sense a tone of mockery in his response? It was hard to tell.

"Julian! Julian Sharpe!"

Julian looked up, as she did, as a thin, lanky young man in a stylish jacket over velvet slacks stopped by the table. Kelly sensed immediately that he was another entertainer of some sort. He seemed both surprised and awed to see Julian. The two men shook hands, and Julian introduced Kelly.

"This is Matt Jacobi, one of the best escape artists this side of the Rockies," Julian said.

Under His Spell

"Flatterer," the young man scoffed, grinning. "Lady, do you know that you're dining out with a living legend?"

"Now who's flattering?" Julian said with a wince. "Though I'm not sure about the compliment—living legends are usually a little long in the tooth."

"C'mon, Sharpe, you know you're the best. Is Jim here, too?"

"No, he's back at the farm. Are you playing in town?"

As the two men began to talk shop, Kelly excused herself and made a quick trip to the ladies' room. She was familiar with this sort of male-camaraderie-on-the-road from her days with Richard, as well. One thing she recognized now though: Julian was obviously well regarded by his peers. The younger man's deference and awe, the affection from a prominent pop star... Though one wouldn't know it from his reserved magician's manner, he was apparently a celebrity to be reckoned with.

When she returned to the table, the younger performer was seated by Julian, who seemed especially absorbed in what he was saying. Julian turned to her when she sat down, a look of aroused interest in his face. "We're going to make a little detour," he announced. "I've just learned of a most interesting place where we can spend the night."

"Oh? Where's that?"

"Hammond," Matt volunteered. "Just a bit south of here."

"Matt's been telling me about a beautiful mansion out in the suburbs there," Julian said. "Six bedrooms, Old World elegance, sculpted gardens—and we'd have it all to ourselves."

"Really?" She looked from one man to the other, sensing something in their expressions that provoked her suspicions. "Whose is it?"

"An acquaintance of Matt's," Julian said. "But he's not in it presently."

"Nope," Matt said gravely, shaking his head. "Couldn't handle it."

"What do you mean?" she asked. "What's wrong with it?"

"Probably nothing," Julian said with a faint smile.

"Enough nothing to send him packing," Matt muttered.

"I don't get it," Kelly said. "Is the house unsafe?"

Julian chuckled. "I'm sure it's safe," he said with a glance at his companion. "But according to rumor"—he shook his head—"it's haunted."

"You know, I was just starting to respect you," Kelly said crossly, arms folded as she peered into the darkness surrounding the road ahead. "I was beginning to think of you as a mature and responsible individual—"

"Thank you," Julian murmured, flicking on his high beams.

"—who was above such juvenile pursuits and harebrained schemes—"

"Hold on, there's a dip ahead."

"—as hunting up ghosts in the dead of night, but obviously—"

"Hold on—"

"—your idea of a good time is—oof!" Only Julian's forearm across her chest kept Kelly from pitching forward as the bus trundled noisily over a bad patch of rolling road. The increased palpitations of her heart at his assured and casually intimate hold on her made her irritation flare.

"Do you mind?" She removed his hand from just over her breast.

"Not at all," he cracked, with an impish smile. "You were saying?"

"I was saying that your idea of a fun way to spend the evening is just plain dumb," she fumed, holding onto the edges of her seat as the bus hugged a sharp curve.

"Well, to tell you the truth, Kelly, my main concern is getting a good night's sleep," he said mildly. "That couch back there gives me a stiff back, if you must know, and if we've got the keys—"

"Sorry to inconvenience you," she muttered.

"—to a house full of big, soft, four-poster beds, I don't see why we should pass up the opportunity of sleeping in style."

"Your friend's friend didn't get much sleep there."

"Matt's buddy's just a superstitious old—" The rumble of the motor covered his murmured expletive. "He's probably just suffused with guilt because he got the house for a song when the old lady passed away."

"What did she die of? Fright?"

Julian chuckled. "Old age." He glanced at her, shaking his head. "Kelly Robbins, I'm surprised at you—scared of a few things that go bump in the night?"

Kelly cleared her throat, her eyes on the road. She wasn't about to tell him that this dashing, worldly reporter for a sophisticated metropolitan magazine had been so frightened of the dark as a child that she still slept with a night light on.

"I'm not scared," Kelly said defensively. "I'm just . . . good Lord!" she exclaimed, peering through the windshield. "Is that it? It looks like the house from *Psycho!*"

The winding private road had ended in a circular driveway, and the Muggeridge mansion, all five Victorian gables and three floors of it, was silhouetted against the three-quarter moon and wisps of silver clouds. It did indeed resemble the homes of movie nightmares, and Kelly couldn't repress a shudder at its imposing, shadowy aura in the sudden silence of the night as Julian cut the motor.

"Nice," he observed laconically. "Must be at least seventy years old."

"It probably has rats and bats," Kelly said.

"Siegfried's good with rats," Julian said cheerily, as if that should assuage any of her apprehensions. "Come on."

Only the quiet chirp of crickets in the surrounding bushes disturbed the stillness of the air as Kelly followed Julian up the front steps. The door swung open with a loud creak when he unlocked it. Kelly involuntarily stiffened and hung back, rubbing her bare arms against the cool night air. Then, with a deliberately careless toss of her head, she followed him staunchly inside.

It was too dark to see much of the interior. She could hear Julian searching for a light switch, heard the click when he found it—but no light went on.

"Right," he said. "Electricity's been turned off. Well, that's no problem..."

"Where are you going?" she said in alarm, as he moved to the door.

"I've got some candles in the bus."

"I'll go with you."

She could see his smile broaden in the dim light. "Didn't realize you were liking my company so much."

Kelly ignored him, stepped back to the door, and emerged into the open air. Julian bounded down the steps to the bus and she followed slowly, folding her arms against the wind that had come up. It rattled a shutter somewhere on the mansion's somber face, and various creaks and rustles reached her ears from all around the looming building.

The jingle of Siegfried's silver chain from the bus's interior was a more comforting sound. Julian appeared with the leopard in tow, and some long white candles in his hand. Head down, Siegfried sniffed the overgrown grass at the edge of the driveway, growled, then padded obediently after his master up the porch steps. Kelly followed close behind.

Once inside, Julian lit two candles, handing Kelly one. There appeared to be a draft in the house, as Kelly's candle went out almost immediately. She was about to call out, stopping in her tracks, when the flame magically sputtered back on.

"They don't go out," Julian explained, his voice seeming to boom with unnatural volume in the cavernous hallway. "Stage candles."

"Oh," she said, her own voice sounding high-pitched and tremulous to her. Kelly cleared her throat. "I hope they've got linens," she said, affecting a casual tone. The flickering candle was casting eerie shadows on the old wallpapered walls on either side of her as she followed Julian and Siegfried toward a large staircase. What she could see of the interior was surprisingly clean and unshabby: old carpeting that was worn but unstained, lighting fixtures that were relatively modern. Large bulky shapes cloaked in ghostly white gave her a heart-stopping start when she glanced into what was apparently the living room. Then she realized, as Siegfried growled, and turned in her direction, that the furniture was covered with sheets.

"Plenty of linen there," Julian remarked, amused. "But according to Matt, the upstairs has everything—clean sheets, blankets, towels. His friend moved out only a few weeks ago and he hasn't even begun to clear the place out of his belongings."

"You mean he left in a big hurry."

Julian chuckled. The stairs creaked softly under his feet. A gust of wind blew both their candles out, and Kelly froze in midstep. Somewhere upstairs a door slammed shut with a resounding crack. She felt her heart hammer in her chest.

"I think," Julian said evenly, as their candles flickered, sputtered, and slowly lit once more, "that the last tenant left a window open."

"Uh-huh," was all Kelly could manage. Siegfried jingled his chain impatiently, pausing at the top of the staircase.

"Are you all right?" Julian was looking at her with concern.

"Certainly," she said, taking the next few steps a bit more quickly. "I don't see any ghosts," she added, with forced breeziness. "Do you?"

Julian smiled. "The only thing that looks ghostly around here is your complexion," he said wryly, and yawned. "Come on, let's find the bedrooms."

He was indicating that she should lead. Kelly hesitated, peering into the darkness above the stairwell.

"Something wrong?"

Kelly steeled herself for the climb, determined not to show a trace of fear.

"Maybe you'd rather sleep out in the bus," he said.

The thought of descending once more into the house's lower depths and being alone in the bus outside was enough to send shivers down her spine. "No, thanks," she said tersely. "It's so much more fun being here with you."

Julian chuckled at her sarcastic tone, then paused at a doorway on their left. "Here's one bedroom," he said, peering within. "Just a mattress, though—let's see what else is in this wing."

Further explorations brought them to a bedroom that adjoined another through a shared bathroom. In one there was a made bed and other evidences of recent occupation. Julian hunted them up some clean sheets and blankets from a cupboard by the bathroom.

"I still don't see," Kelly muttered, as Julian helped her make the bed, "why you're so interested in a house like this. If your back's out of whack, we could've traded places, you know. I'd be glad to sleep on the couch—"

"Never!" said Julian, with mock indignation. "Besides, I get a kick out of challenging the so-called Spirit World. I'll take on any spook—with one hand tied behind my back," he added loudly, as if for the benefit of any lurking apparitions.

"You could be asking for trouble," Kelly murmured. Julian's face was close to hers now as they tucked the blankets in from opposite sides of the bed. He raised his eyebrow roguishly at her remark.

"Maybe you'd rather not sleep alone," he suggested.

Kelly looked into his openly suggestive eyes and felt a tremor of answering arousal at the undisguised desire she saw there. But the mockery in his tone brought her to her senses. "I'll be fine," she said coolly. "Besides, wasn't the whole idea that you should have a nice big bed to stretch out in? I wouldn't think of cramping you."

Julian grinned. "On the contrary," he said. "Having a warm, soft body beside one makes for the sweetest dreams..."

Kelly straightened up, tugging the covers into place, hoping that the darkness would disguise the flush she felt in her cheeks as Julian's seductive imagery registered within her. "Maybe Siegfried'll help you out," she said dryly. "But I'll be fine right here."

Julian sighed. "Somehow it wouldn't be the same," he said. "Besides, Sig's got to stand guard." Julian had tied the end of the leopard's chain to his bedroom doorknob, and the big cat was sprawled comfortably in the hall. Julian

Under His Spell

strode to the door now and closed it. As he turned back to Kelly, it creaked open again.

"Latch doesn't work," he said, frowning. "Well, Sig'll do a security check on any unwelcome visitors."

Kelly watched him carefully shut the door again. The simple domestic act of making the bed had helped dispel her apprehensive feelings for the moment, but as she listened to the rustle of tree branches outside her curtained window, those feelings returned full force.

"Well, if the walking dead come out of the closet or something, I'm just on the other side." Julian smiled, patting the freshly made bed. With that cheery remark he turned, taking his candle, and walked into the bathroom, shutting the door behind him.

She wanted to call out for him to leave the adjoining door open, but she controlled herself with an effort. Let's be practical, she told herself. You never believed in ghosts before, and with a guard like Siegfried on one side and Julian on the other... Her eyes were drawn against her will to the closet door, set in the wall's dark mahogany paneling across from the bed. Damn that man! she cursed silently, as shadows shifted in the lone candle's flicker. Why did he have to mention the closet?

She awoke with a start sometime later and sat bolt upright in the bed. Some noise had pulled her abruptly from sleep and she strained to hear it now, clutching the covers to her bosom. What had it been?

The branches she'd noticed earlier rustled again. Somewhere above her a floorboard creaked and she stiffened, immediately imagining phantom footsteps. But none followed. Something was different about the room, though. It took her a moment to realize that the faithful candle Julian had stuck with wax to her night table had finally sputtered out.

Another creak. Kelly's eyes shifted to the door. The door was moving.

Horrified, she watched, pulse pounding, as it ever so

slowly opened of its own accord. She opened her mouth. Nothing came out. The door was halfway open—three quarters—

Suddenly it swung noiselessly shut, with a muffled click. Kelly swallowed. A draft. It had to be. That was the only rational reason for... a knocking? From *inside* the closet?

Kelly stared at the closet door, goosebumps breaking out all over her skin. A dull thud... thud... thud... came from within the closet, as if—the thought was terrifying—there was... something in there, trying to get out...

She couldn't take her eyes away from the closet door until the noise abated. Then she turned to the bathroom door, mentally measuring the distance from bed to door. Merely a few yards' leap, she decided, and that was the best course. If she was very quiet, and moved very slowly...

Then she heard the other noise, and realized with a shiver of fear that this was what had awakened her. It was a voice. Wasn't it?

Yet there was no other way to describe it. The low, prolonged, and hair-raising moan came from the wall directly behind her bed's headboard. Frozen in the act of lifting the covers, Kelly listened with rising hysteria as the unearthly moan grew louder. It was a horrible, tortured sound, like the asthmatic, pained wheezing of an old woman...

The wind rose, bringing on a chorus of creaks and rustlings to augment the ghostly crying in the wall. Kelly's blood was turning to ice.

Then the door swung open with a *crack!* and she was in the air.

She got from her bed to the bathroom door, through the bathroom and the door to Julian's room as if shot from a cannon, her trajectory sending her right into the bed. Its occupant stiffened with a murmured noise of protest as she clung on, a shivering, shaken bundle of frayed nerves. Then Julian turned instinctively to take her into his strong, warm arms.

"Mmm," he said, in a husky voice thick with sleep. "It's about time..."

"Julian!" she hissed through clenched teeth. "Wake up!"

Under His Spell 77

"H...umph," he muttered, hugging her lazily to his stretched-out frame. "...smell good..."

"Wake up!" She shook him until his eyes snapped open.

"What's a matter?" he mumbled.

"There's something in there," she whispered, as he stared at her, uncomprehending. "There's something in the closet and there's someone in the wall!"

"In the wall?" She nodded, as he rubbed the back of his thumb across his cheek, and yawned. Then, as he put his arm around her again, obviously not intending to move, Kelly realized that Julian Sharpe slept in the nude. His lean and naked body was wrapped around her in an intimate embrace. She could feel the stirrings of his aroused interest as she moved her legs against his in an attempt to gain her balance—a move he seemed to misinterpret, as he tightened his hold instead of loosening it. Half asleep, his motor was already revving up.

"Listen!" she hissed, forcibly pushing him away from her. He scowled, shifting his weight to one elbow, and dutifully cocked his head as she gestured wildly toward her room with her hand.

There it was again, audible through the opened doors— the low, keening moan that rose and crested in a louder groan as they listened, still in the darkness. Julian sat up in bed.

"Interesting," he muttered.

"Interesting?!" She stared from him to the doorway.

"Hand me my robe, will you?"

"No!" she whispered, unwilling to relinquish his company just yet. "What are you doing?"

He shrugged. "Okay, don't hand me my robe."

Before she could stop him, he was rising from the bed. Kelly caught a glimpse of his bronzed, muscular nakedness in motion as he climbed over her, his broad back and firm, taut buttocks, before he slipped the robe on and turned back in her direction, tying it closed. Even while shivering with fear, she was aware of the warm tingle of excitement this view of his bared anatomy provoked in her.

"Stay there," he whispered softly.

"No problem," she whispered back, huddling under the sheets.

She watched him walk through the bathroom into her bedroom. Through the open doorways she could glimpse him leaning against the wall, tapping on the paneling, bending down to examine the space beneath the bed. Then, as she craned her neck to see what he was doing, he disappeared from view.

She waited. He didn't reappear. "Julian!" she hissed. No answer.

A minute that felt like ten passed. She called his name again. But he had obviously left the other room. The voice had died down, but as she listened, it was starting up again. When Julian still didn't appear, she began to panic.

One thing was certain. She wasn't about to lie here with that door open. Gingerly she pulled back the covers. Slowly, she tiptoed to the bathroom door. Staring at the darkness beyond the bathroom, ready to bolt at any movement from within there, she began to close the bathroom door.

When she felt the hand on her shoulder Kelly let loose with the scream she'd been building up to for the last twenty minutes. Julian clapped his hands to his ears—it was, of course, he who'd come up behind her—and Siegfried padded through the bedroom doorway, ears bristling, eyes glowing with annoyance. Julian calmed him down, and then led Kelly, unprotesting, to the bed, where only his most persistent, gently soothing strokes on her shivering shoulders brought her back to sanity.

"I was checking the room on the other side of yours," he explained. "I think what we've got here is a case of bad plumbing."

"Plumbing?" She shot him a glance over her shoulder, as she huddled in a little ball, her back to him beneath the covers.

"I mean it's the pipes," he said, with obvious amusement. "That's not a human voice. It's the wind going through valves and such. This whole place is draft crazy. Look, you didn't hear it saying words to you, right?"

"Sure I did," she muttered, "It said, 'Get the hell out of

Under His Spell

this house before your hair turns white!'"

Julian chuckled. "I'll take a more thorough look around in the morning. But I assure you, there's nobody in your room. You can go back now, it's safe—honestly."

"Not on your life," she said. "I'm not moving."

"Suit yourself," he said. "That's fine with me."

As he settled himself under the covers next to her, she mentally prepared some speech telling him to keep his hands off, not get the wrong idea, maintain a reasonable distance... But his body felt good beside hers, warm and comforting, and when he casually slipped an arm around her with a muffled yawn, the words all evaporated from her mind.

"Good night, then," he murmured.

She mumbled a good-night, too, but her eyes were wide open. The phantom voice in the wall was indistinguishable, with both doors shut, and even the darkness around her had lost most of its menacing look as she lay in the secure shelter of his arms, so it wasn't fear that kept her awake—at least not fear of the supernatural.

No, it was a different fear... Now that she was suddenly in bed with Julian, his body nestled close to hers, she was aware of a simmering, zinging sensation in her blood. Her nerve endings had become sensitized. As she shifted nervously in Julian's embrace, the natural slope of the soft bedding brought her even more snugly against him, and she could feel every contour of his leonine length.

The bed was heady with his masculine scent. Fighting the heat that was slowly enveloping her, she exhaled a deep breath. Julian languidly slipped his arm around her side, the steady warmth of his breath on her neck tickling her skin enticingly. The soft pressure of his arm beneath her breasts filled her body with a delicious ache.

Sleep! she commanded herself, though she knew it was impossible. As she moved again, her whole body too electrically charged to remain still, his lips gently nuzzled the back of her neck and his arm rose slightly, ever so gently nudging the bottoms of her breasts beneath the sheer pajamas she wore. Vivid images of his tawny nudity, glimpsed earlier, filled her mind. Lying there was becoming torturous.

She heard the wind come up again outside, and the door that had slammed before creaked again. Involuntarily, her body stiffened, and she turned toward Julian. His eyes were half closed, heavy-lidded with... sleep? Or desire? His lips looked invitingly soft, only inches from hers. His hand had shifted subtly to caress her side as she turned to face him, trembling with an expectancy only fueled by fear.

"You don't look sleepy," he murmured huskily, his eyes gleaming in the darkness. "In fact, with the way you're looking right now, I don't feel sleepy myself..."

He bent his face closer to hers. Kelly moved hers back an inch. "What... way I'm looking?" she whispered apprehensively, her heart beginning to race at the magnetic sensuality in his gaze.

"A little breathless..." he whispered, the hint of a smile lifting the tips of his mustache. "A little vulnerable..." He touched her chin lightly with his forefinger and softly, slowly traced the line of her jaw, sending a delicious tremor through her body from head to foot. "... and very, very beautiful," he finished softly, gently cupping her chin now between thumb and forefinger.

"Now *you're* seeing things," she whispered, aware that she probably looked like a nervous wreck.

"Umm," he whispered, in a husky rumble, his fingers softly stroking her cheek. "I'm seeing the most gorgeous vision..."

"This is... rank flattery," she whispered, trying desperately to keep herself from falling under the spell of his skin-tingling caress, and the sultry glow of his dark eyes in the dim moonlight.

"No," he whispered. "It's the truth..."

His face hovered closer. Her entire body seemed to throb in his embrace. Mounting arousal threatened to overcome all her thoughts of breaking loose. She felt herself falling, slipping into a caldron of simmering sensation.

"Why... are we whispering?" she whispered weakly.

He nodded almost imperceptibly. "Let's stop," he murmured.

And then his mouth closed over hers. The gentle pressure of his warm lips sent a tendril of flame through her. Her lips parted of their own volition as his tongue entered, touching hers. She lost herself in the erotic pulse of their deepening kiss. His hand at her side moved to cup her breast lightly, and she felt its tip swell and stiffen at his caress.

Desire flared and deepened within her so fast that she was breathless as he pressed her tight against his thighs, and a moan broke from her lips. Their tongues danced and meshed. Instinctively, she brought her arms around his strong shoulders, her breasts pressing now against his smooth, hard chest—

The loud slam of a door abruptly broke the spell of desire. Heart pounding, she pushed desperately loose from his embrace, her head whipping around to face the door.

"You see?" she whispered shakily. "There it is—"

"I see..." he said, his voice smoldering and low. "I'm only seeing beauty in the night..." His fingers were playing with her hair, playfully pulling her back to the pillow.

"No," she murmured, her breath still fast, her nerves on edge. The combination of Julian's arousing kiss and the sudden fright had keyed her up to the height of anxiety. "This is... I can't—"

"Kelly," he said soothingly, "there's nothing to be afraid of."

Above them, somewhere, another door creaked loudly and clicked closed in the stillness. Kelly sat up in the bed, protectively hugging her chest with her arms. Julian lay back against the pillow with a resigned sigh.

"I'm sorry," she mumbled. "But... this is all wrong, anyway... I didn't come in here to..." Her voice trailed off lamely. How did she ever end up here like this, stuck in bed with Julian Sharpe in a haunted house in the wilds of Illinois?

"I know," he said quietly, his eyes holding hers, still gleaming with unconcealed desire. "But that doesn't make it wrong."

The wind rose again, bringing the house alive once more with little noises inside and out. Kelly shivered involuntarily, and looked away. "Julian," she said softly, "I . . . liked having you kiss me . . . But in the first place, it shouldn't happen again, and in the second place, this isn't the place—" She stopped, embarrassed, her own words sounding absurd to her.

He chuckled softly in the darkness. "I can understand that imaginary spooks and spirits don't do wonders for losing one's inhibitions," he said. "But why don't you lie down again? I'm sure I could help you forget about—"

"Sorry," she said quickly. "But I've been forgetting too much as it is. We've got a professional relationship to maintain, you and I. Remember?"

"Oh, that," he said airily. "Aren't you being a little too—"

"Uh-uh," she said firmly, bridling at his arrogant tone. *"You're* being a little too . . ." The creak of the door in the next room grabbed her attention. His widening smile as she stiffened back against the headboard was even more maddening.

"Look," she said. "You go to sleep. I'm going to sit here and look out for . . . for . . ."

"Yes?" He grinned.

"Myself," she said crossly. "If anything weird happens, you'll be the first to know. Okay?"

He nodded with mock seriousness, settling back against his pillow. "I still think you look beautiful when you're frightened," he murmured.

Kelly shot him a withering glance. "Good night," she said.

"'Night."

Kelly stared at the closed door. So far, there was one consistent characteristic about her life with Julian Sharpe: she should never assume she'd get a decent night's sleep.

Chapter 5

WITH SUNLIGHT STREAMING in through the windows the following morning, her bedroom didn't look at all foreboding. Still, Kelly kept her distance as Julian approached the closet door. He paused, listening as she did to the dull knocking sound from within.

"Here goes nothing," he muttered, then pulled open the door.

Kelly's hand was over her eyes. In the silence that followed, she slowly widened her fingers to get a look. An old-fashioned metal "shoe tree" hung from the sole hanger in the musky interior. As she watched, it swung gently forward of its own volition, then back.

Julian folded his arms, then shook his head, amused. "Matt's friend's a damned fool. I'm sure there are more knocks and creaks and noises in the house than there should be—and why not? There's not a floor that's level in the whole place, and the wind's getting in through every crack—this is no mansion, it's a wooden sieve!"

"What did you find in the cellar?" she asked, peering over his shoulder as he pointed out a loose board in the closet's back and held his hand out, testing the draft that she, too, could feel.

"Just like I thought," he said. "Bad plumbing. Your ghost in the wall is a pipe in the wall that's badly in need of replacement. And there's a big enough family of squirrels in the attic to account for any of the scurrying night noises he was talking about..."

"I guess imagination's a powerful thing," she said as he shut the closet door and moved across the room to collect the last of their belongings.

"You said it," he sighed. "That's Wolfgang Lang's biggest asset—everybody else's gullibility."

She watched in silence as he stuffed his robe into the bag he'd brought with them the night before, feeling doubly foolish now in the light of day.

"But I wouldn't have missed last night for anything," he went on, as if eavesdropping on her private thoughts.

"Oh, really?" She avoided his amused glance.

"Got a great night's sleep," he said cheerfully. "And such good company! You know, I could really get used to a sleeping arrangement like that. What would you think about, say, tonight—"

"Like I said, Julian," she retorted, "imagination's a potent thing. Yours is wildly out of line."

"And I suppose I imagined," he began, his eyes twinkling devilishly, "that you didn't exactly mind the position you were in..."

"If you're packed, we should really be going," she said, turning resolutely to the door. "Don't we have a long day's driving ahead of us?"

"After you," he said politely, with an expansive sweep of his arm.

Kelly headed down the hall, ignoring the little flip-flops her stomach insisted on doing as images of their brief embrace flickered all too vividly in her mind. At least today, she mused wryly, his hands would be on the wheel... And at least, she had to admit, he'd been decent enough to refrain from pointing out how foolishly she'd behaved last night...

"I think we've seen the last of corn," said Kelly, peering out the side window. "That is, we have, haven't we? My eyes are starting to turn green."

"They're green already, aren't they?" Julian commented, reaching above him to take a pair of sunglasses down. The late afternoon sun was shining directly in their eyes as the road stretched on into Nebraska.

"So they tell me," she said. "How far from here to your farm?"

"About fifty miles," he said laconically. "Getting fidgety?"

"I guess," she admitted. "Between the pages of print and the fields of corn... —she yawned—"... and the miles of highway..." She yawned again.

"That's pretty poetic," said Julian. "Did you ever think of doing any writing?"

"Funny guy," said Kelly. "All right. This is positively the last article I'm going to read. From here on out, if there's something I'm supposed to know that I haven't learned already, it's just... too bad."

She opened the magazine in her lap—the current issue of *Magic Manuscript,* a bi-monthly publication of "the world's largest magic store," in New York City—and examined the glossy page Julian had earmarked for her to read. The jingle of a chain behind her told her that Siegfried was out for his afternoon stroll. Now that the animal was used to Kelly's presence, and vice versa, Julian let it roam freely through the trailer as they traveled. When Siegfried sat between them, looking balefully from Julian to Kelly, she didn't even think twice before giving the leopard's mane an affectionate pat.

"What's a 'vernet'?" she asked Julian.

"Fake thumb," he said, his slightly oblique reply indicating she was treading on secret territory. In the few days they'd been traveling together, Kelly could already intuit from the magician's tone how detailed an answer he was willing to accord a question. Monosyllabic rejoinders meant to ask no further. Short phrases indicated that, if pressed, he'd say more. Smiles and chuckles were his tacit admission that she'd surmised something on her own that required some ingenuity or imagination.

"Do you use fake thumbs?"

He cocked his head slightly, which usually meant: yes, but there's more to it than you need to know.

"Well, does Wolfgang Lang use them?"

Julian pursed his lips thoughtfully. "Not to my knowledge," he said. "He does too much close-up work. Even a good fake thumb tip's too easily spotted, if your audience is right on top of you."

Kelly nodded, then continued reading. Ever since they'd gotten back on the road early that morning, soon leaving ghosts and Illinois far behind, she'd been content to stick to conversations dealing strictly with magic, craft, and fakery. She'd dressed down again, to simple khaki shorts and a light short-sleeved blouse, and had maintained a businesslike air throughout the day. She didn't want Julian to get the idea that their brief, intimate encounter the night before had changed anything between them.

It had, though. Kelly bit her lip thoughtfully as her eyes went unconsciously to Julian's profile. Every now and then she'd find herself back there, suddenly—trembling with heated arousal in Julian's arms... remembering with sinful clarity the first time he'd kissed her—and it took an almost superhuman effort to return to reality once her imagination began to take her further. Every casual look, touch, the incidental brushing against him as she took her seat, set off little sparks of sensual awareness in her now. There was no mistaking the symptoms; Kelly knew herself too well. She was...

Infatuated, leave it at that. Well, such things were bound to happen, she told herself philosophically. He was an uncommonly attractive man; she'd been alone too long, it seemed now, and after all, he was so openly flirtatious—

Kelly frowned. But that was the other thing that had changed. Julian had, well, shifted somehow in his attitude. It was subtle, but she could sense it. He no longer jokingly came on to her, or tried to make each harmless remark the pretext of an erotic double entendre. There was a slight reserve in his manner that was throwing her off. Could it be that her constant rebuffs had finally penetrated, and he'd conceded romantic defeat? Doubtful. Or, worse, did he somehow know that his attractiveness had finally penetrated *her* defenses, and that he didn't need to press his advantage?

The thought of being so consciously manipulated made her squirm. She was probably blowing everything out of proportion, she decided; most likely his thoughts were al-

Under His Spell

together elsewhere—on the convention ahead, or the farm, or his tour, or his...

Girl friends? With an inward groan, Kelly turned the magazine page, determined not to dwell upon the question that had begun to plague her, at odd moments: Did Julian really lead the kind of life Richard had led, full of casual conquests from town to town? After her oft-repeated stance about not delving into personal matters, it was the last question she'd ever ask him, of course. But when she thought about it, he'd been vague and seemingly ironic about "dating" when the topic had come up in their earlier conversation...

Why are you thinking about it at all? she asked herself, exasperated, and turned the magazine page so violently she nearly ripped it. Then a name printed in boldface there caught her eye. "Say, Julian—this 'Sharpe effect' they're talking about—is that you?"

Julian nodded. Kelly read the paragraph with renewed interest. Many famous magicians who had developed unique, breakthrough techniques had earned their place in magic history in this manner—there was "the Dunninger technique," "the Wilson sleight"—and now this, a reference to Julian and James Sharpe's "disappearing beast illusion."

"What is the Sharpe effect?" she asked.

Julian smiled. "You'll see," he said, "maybe when we get to the farm."

But the first truly affecting sight Kelly saw, when they pulled up to the Sharpe homestead just before sundown, was the tall, lanky, robustly handsome man who was obviously James Sharpe. Smiling wide, his surprising blond hair glinting bronze in the deepening sunset, he bounded down the front steps of the sprawling farmhouse as Julian pulled up in a cloud of dust.

When Julian opened the bus door, his brother's exclamation of greeting was cut short by Siegfried. The big cat, clearly excited to see his other master, nearly knocked him backward as he leaped from the captivity of the trailer, putting his paws on James's shoulders and nuzzling his face.

"Down, fella!" James laughed, playfully nudging the beast's face from side to side with a closed fist. Siegfried let out what sounded like a happy roar and dropped to the ground, rubbing his tawny length against James's side. "Well!" James said expansively, his bright blue eyes widening with interest as Kelly alighted from the bus. "Here's an unexpected pleasure—who's your friend, Julian?"

"Kelly Robbins—James Sharpe, my other half. I won't say better," he muttered, with a chuckle, as James took her hand and gave it an emphatic squeeze.

"Where'd he find you?" asked James. "Not in the low-class joints he usually gets thrown out of, I'm sure—" He grinned, ducking a punch from his brother, who glowered in mock indignation.

"Don't listen to a word this man says," Julian said wryly. "Kelly is the journalist I told you about," he went on, as James continued to give her a frank appraisal with his laughing eyes. "She's going to Denver with me to lay traps for Wolfgang Lang—"

"Julian! And in time for dinner, for a change!"

Kelly turned as the feminine and distinctly Southern voice sailed across the yard. A stunningly attractive woman whose short skirt and tight halter top only accentuated her shapely legs and curvaceous figure strode briskly down the front porch steps and directly into Julian Sharpe's arms.

Only after she'd hugged the tall magician, given him a peck on the cheek, beaming, and then returned to James's side did Kelly find her breath coming a little easier. As James put his arm casually around the young woman, whom he introduced as Annie, Kelly reflected, helplessly, that the seething surge of jealousy she'd just felt was entirely unfounded.

"Annie's been cooking her special chicken," James announced. "But you don't get any, bro, until you see what Theo's been cooking up in the barn. It's monstrous, man—his most fiendish creation yet!"

He was already leading Julian away, leaving the two women to face each other as the leopard bounded after the men. Annie rolled her eyes at James's excited ravings and

Under His Spell 89

wild gesticulations, and gave Kelly a friendly smile. "Are you staying overnight? I mean, do you have bags?"

"Yes, I do," Kelly said.

"Need a hand?" Kelly shook her head. "Well, bring your stuff in—I have to check on the corn. Why don't you meet me in the kitchen and we'll find a room for you."

Kelly thanked her and went back to the bus to unload her gear. When she emerged, the sun was a red ball on the horizon behind the house. She paused a moment to drink in the view. In the flurry of their arrival, she hadn't had a chance to really appreciate the Sharpe brothers' homestead. Now she let her eyes travel slowly over the picturesque vista.

The farmhouse stood alone, a quaintly ramshackle but brightly painted building that hearkened back another century or so in feeling, the one structure visible, except for a large barn to her right, for miles. On all sides of her were rolling fields, purpling now with the sun's descent: a distant forest with a flying V of blackbirds above, a winding fence glinting faintly in the sun's last rays. The caws of the birds, the soft whisper of the wind, and sounds of silverware and crockery emanating from the kitchen's curtained window were the only sounds.

The sky above her, vast and deeply darkening blue, seemed tremendous. The land seemed to stretch forever, to infinity. Kelly sighed, her heart suddenly aching with a mixture of joy and nostalgia. When was the last time she'd been on land so huge, in air so pure, with no skyscrapers, smog, streetlights, or sirens to hem her in on every side?

Just as suddenly, she was grateful Julian had brought her here into the heartland. One tended to forget, she mused wryly, slowly walking up the wooden steps of the farmhouse's porch, how rich the "emptiness" out here really was, rich with colors, smells, and an exhilarating sense of freedom. With an affectionate glance at the porch swing and antique rocking chair that creaked quietly in the breeze, she opened the screen door and went on into the kitchen.

Annie was leaning over the oven, peering in at a chicken

whose smell was mouth-wateringly delectable. Hearing Kelly enter, she stood up, slamming the oven door with a bang. "Hope you're not a vegetarian." She grinned. Kelly shook her head, and the taller woman led the way up carpeted stairs to a landing, where she paused uncertainly.

"Julian's room is over here, but, um, if you'd rather have your own..."

"I would," Kelly said and, feeling for some reason that she should justify her presence, began to explain her mission as Annie led her down the hall. Annie listened with what seemed like genuine interest, but her attitude conveyed that anybody was entitled to do whatever he or she felt like doing, in her book. Urging Kelly to join her downstairs soon, Annie left her.

A few crows seated outside her window flew away at Kelly's approach. Wind chimes hanging there tinkled softly. The room was a small, cozy melange of country bric-a-brac, complete with calico quilt and a cedarwood chest at the foot of the four-poster bed. Kelly loved every inch of the homey room. It reminded her of her house in Maine. Even the eaved ceiling made her feel like the child she'd been there; her bedroom in Kennebunkport had been under the roof as well.

For the first time since leaving the city, she unpacked her bag, having noticed a cedar closet and deciding she could put it to good use. But when she laid out the items she'd hurriedly packed, they suddenly seemed oddly inappropriate to her atop the country quilt. City clothes, she mused, conscious now of how the stylish, fashionable things she'd taken to wearing were markedly man-tailored. Their unprovocative cuts always made her feel protected and authoritative in the office. But out here...

The only ultra-feminine apparel she'd packed was a sheer and billowy loose silk blouse of pale rose color. Its extra length and nearly see-through thinness had relegated it to infrequent use, and she wasn't quite sure why she'd brought it along. Impulsively, Kelly decided now that the casually sexy, carefree attitude the blouse exuded was just right for her mood. And the one skirt she'd thrown in as a sop to

Under His Spell 91

summer white—hardly ever worn on the job because it hugged her curves like a second skin—had found its moment as well.

After a quick, refreshing shower in the antique tub in the adjoining blondwood bathroom, she put on her "new look" and headed downstairs, where the scents of cornbread, corn, and chicken mingled invitingly as she approached the kitchen. Annie had just finished setting the table.

"Need any help?" Annie shook her head, and gave her the once-over with a friendly smile. "Well, it looks like you've scrubbed the road off."

Kelly smiled back. "That shower was wonderful." She paused at the door. "This is a great house."

"Don't you love it?" Annie nodded. "You ought to take a walk around after dinner. The land just goes for miles."

Something in Annie's carefree and friendly manner made exchanging confidences seem only natural. "I miss this kind of space," she said. "Are you out here all year round?"

Annie shrugged. "I've known the guys for only a little while. I work with them now, you know—in their act. So we travel most of the time. This is the longest stretch of being in one place so far, since I've been with Jim. Next tour doesn't start till summer's over." She smiled. "I don't know if Jim can handle it, to tell you the truth. He's used to bein' on the move."

"They're different, aren't they?" Kelly ventured. "Jim and Julian."

Annie blew a wisp of brown hair out of her eyes, lifting the lid off a steaming pot of corn. "Well, Jim's louder." She laughed. "And blonder. And I guess he's not so... serious, in a way. But they're brothers, all right. You can tell." She turned the flame off and deftly forked a cob out into a bowl. "Are you a wine drinker? Or beer?"

"Wine, I guess," Kelly told her. She hovered in the doorway, wanting to ask Annie more questions. But not wanting to appear too nosy, she paused. Annie looked up.

"Hate beer," she said. Then, holding Kelly's eyes for a beat longer than she had before, she asked, casually, "Julian been good company?"

"Well, I—I guess so," Kelly said.

"Hmm," said Annie, with a faint smile. "He's a little hard to reach, if you ask me."

Kelly smiled, warming to Annie's forthright manner. "How long have you and James been... together?"

Annie screwed her eyes up at the ceiling. "A couple of months, I guess." A sputter of grease from the oven's interior distracted her. "If you do want to help, just go get those lunkheads out of the barn in another minute," she said sardonically, opening the oven door again. "If Theo's got 'em all raveled up in some new invention, they'll forget to eat at all."

"Who is Theo?" Kelly asked, moving to the window. Noises of machinery came faintly from the barn.

"He's the whiz kid," Annie said, peering into the oven's interior. "Still in high school, but a regular Einstein. He's what you'd call a technical mastermind, I guess—sits around staring into space for hours at a time, and then he comes up with a new idea for a trick—usually does it with computers. Julian found him."

"Found him?"

"*Adopted* might be a better word." Annie shut the oven and joined Kelly at the window, turning her face to feel the breeze. "Theodore doesn't have much of a family. His dad's the town drunk. So, when the kid snuck out here one night on one of his many jaunts away from home, Julian took a liking to him and put him to work. He practically lives here now—happy as a pig in..." She paused. "Maybe you ought to fetch 'em now. We're about ready here."

As Kelly walked across the yard to the barn, she mulled over her conversation with Annie. She felt almost envious of the woman. Imagine that—to meet a man and be moved in with him, cooking his meals, within two months, and acting so casual about it—all the while knowing it could end just as casually. Kelly shook her head. That was a way she could never be. No, the next time she got involved she wanted the whole deal: marriage, family, the security of setting down roots.

Under His Spell   93

Annie had said the brothers were alike. Kelly could only assume that Julian was as she'd suspected, rootless and liking it, the way James apparently did. But then, she'd never have pictured Julian as the fatherly type, and Annie's story about Theo revealed another side to the man, one Kelly had never seen. How many hidden sides to Julian were there, anyway?

She shook the thought from her mind, annoyed at her constant preoccupation with the hidden character of Julian Sharpe, and opened the barn door, which required a bit of strength. Inside, she stood for a moment in bewilderment and awe.

The barn had been partitioned off into a number of rooms. The one she was in was filled to its two-story ceiling with machinery of all shapes and sizes. From her studies on the magic craft, she understood she was looking at the necessary equipment for large-scale illusions—winches, hydraulics, scaffolded platforms and huge welded metal forms that included some giant magnets. The kind of shows the Sharpe Brothers performed in Vegas necessitated truckloads of the stuff.

To her right was another partitioned-off area that contained backdrops, flats, banks of lights, and sound equipment. She followed her ears to another corner of the barn, where machinery was humming, and a loud whooshing noise threatened to drown out James Sharpe's excited exclamations. Here was a laboratory of sorts, Kelly guessed. She was staring at a bank of computers, a table covered with diagrams, a swinging work light over an opened box of tools sprawled all over the table, bench, and floor. In the midst of it was a wiry, quickly darting figure with curly dark hair and pencils stuck behind both ears, who was an inch shorter than she was. Theo, she surmised. He was talking to someone just outside her line of vision who was obviously on a ladder or something—the small teenager was craning his neck.

Then, as Kelly drew closer, she saw Julian, and her mouth dropped open in amazement. He was sitting in midair, calmly carrying on a conversation as if there was nothing at all peculiar about . . . *floating* was the only word, some eight feet off the ground.

"It holds pretty well," he said to James, who was standing off to his side. "But you'll have to do something about the noise," he added to Theo, who nodded, fiddling with some piece of machinery.

"Let me show you the new ring of fire," Theo said eagerly. "Just keep your hands back a little—"

As Julian complied, the air in front of him was suddenly ablaze with flame. Kelly couldn't suppress a little shriek as the fire seemed to arc in a circle all around Julian, who remained eerily unperturbed, still defying gravity with his legs folded underneath him.

"Just set it off with the proper flourish," James called up to his brother, "and it'll be great. Theo says he's got colors, too."

Nodding, the quick-moving technical whiz adjusted a nozzle above his head, a few feet to the left of the floating Julian, and the flames burst into an electric blue and green ring. Julian nodded, apparently satisfied, then noticed Kelly, and gave her a little wave.

"Hi," he called. "What's up?"

Kelly cleared her throat. "Ah, dinner's ready," she said. "Do you think you could . . ."

"Be right down." He smiled.

"But what I really want," Theo told James excitedly, with a perfunctory polite nod at Kelly, "is to move the ring— you know, and then you—"

Julian shook his head. "Theo," he said patiently, "we tried that. And I nearly burned my—"

"But I've got a better circuit programmed," Theo protested.

"Too complicated," James said.

"That's what you always say," Theo said moodily.

"Listen, Mr. Gadget," said Julian, smiling, "do you know how expensive blowing out that last bank was? Just because you got a little notion—"

"All right, all right, I'll rethink it," Theo muttered. And

Under His Spell

as he pulled a lever on another mysterious machine, Julian began to float slowly down to earth. Kelly watched, fascinated, as he sat up, then stood up, still cushioned by nothing but air. Then his feet hit the metal grating that she noticed beneath him, and he was striding toward her as if he'd never left the ground.

"Uh-uh," he admonished her, as she strained to get a look at whatever it was that had somehow allowed him to "fly." "That's off limits."

As he put his arm around her, leading her from the area, Kelly considered telling him that such familiar gestures were off limits as well, but it seemed silly to protest when she fit so naturally into the curve of his arm. It seemed more a motion of camaraderie than possessiveness, she decided, falling into step with him. But the nearness of him stoked a heat within her body that seemed to answer the warmth of his. By the time they'd reached the open air, a now familiar surge of electricity was pulsing softly beneath her skin.

The words of James and Theo in conversation behind them faded from her consciousness. She was looking at the beauty of the purple-blue sky in the gathering dusk, feeling Julian watching it with her as they walked slowly together in a single rhythm. She was seeing everything around her as if with extra-heightened vision—the farmhouse, as gracefully noble in a homey, unpretentious way as a church in a Grant Wood painting; the rolling fields beyond; and the air that seemed to tingle with life.

"I feel so... alive, out here," she said softly, shivering imperceptibly as he slid his arm tighter around her, hand grazing the curve of her hip.

"Umm," he said. "The air's sweet, isn't it?"

She nodded, inhaling the country mixture of green grass and fresh home cooking. Julian had slowed his pace. Now he halted, as the other two moved past him, into the house, and turned her to look up at him in the darkening shadows.

"That's how you make me feel," he said quietly, his eyes shining with a soft glow. "Alive. More alive than I'm used to feeling."

"Like you're floating on air?" she joked, trying to keep the mood light. Both his hands gently grasped her waist now, and she was fighting a wild impulse to fold right up into his embrace.

"I'm serious," he said, eyes narrowing.

"I'm sorry," she said. "I... I'm glad you like my company," she said awkwardly. "I've been wanting to thank you for... bringing me out here. I've missed these wide open spaces. It's very beautiful here."

"It suits you," he said softly. "The wind in your hair, the smell of the earth..."

Kiss me. Kiss me again, was all she could think, as his eyes traveled languidly over her face and hair. She wanted to be lost in the wonderful feel of him again, to chase her chattering thoughts away, to think of no tomorrows or pasts...

"What are you thinking?" he asked, his voice low and husky.

"I'm thinking... things have gotten personal again," she said, taking a shuddering breath and releasing it. "I didn't want them to..."

He studied her in the half light, as voices raised in carefree bantering floated out over the yard from the kitchen. "Why?" he asked simply. "There's something happening between you and me. You feel it, don't you?"

She swallowed, nodding slowly.

"Then why fight it? Why not seize the moment?"

She stared up at him, confused by the intensity of feelings his gentle grasp created, and the strange conflicting emotions his words evoked. That was what Richard had always said, she realized: Live for now—the rest doesn't matter, the mornings after, the days ahead.

But he'd been wrong! she thought, with an ache of remembrance. It had mattered, all of it, and her life had splintered into painful, jagged pieces when he'd betrayed her so cavalierly. And after every little oasis of passion between them had come a desert of desertion, when he'd gone away, like a wandering minstrel, leaving her to wrestle with the pangs and painful strains of loving, with so little in return...

"I can't," she whispered, feeling trapped beneath his searching gaze.

"You should," he said gently.

"It's easy for you to say," she said, with sudden vehemence, then felt immediately guilty, seeing a look of hurt confusion cross his face, then disappear so quickly she wondered if she'd imagined it.

"Maybe not," was his terse reply. His eyes seemed to glow more fiercely.

Kelly looked away. "Look, I'm sorry—you can see I'm—I'm no good at this," she said. "Couldn't we just keep things—as they are?"

He relaxed his gentle hold on her hips and stepped back, his face in shadow. "If you insist," he said, his voice even but tinged with reluctance.

"Julian, you may be used to casual flirtations—weekend-long relationships—but I'm not . . . that kind of woman," she finished awkwardly.

"You've been pretty quick to peg me as *that* kind of man, I see," he said coolly. "Glad I've made such a trust-inspiring impression."

"I'm sorry," she told him. "I—I'm really having a wonderful time with you. I guess I'm just afraid to . . . mess it up," she added softly.

Julian was silent for a moment. She sensed him measuring her words. "Feelings are messy things, aren't they?" he said at last, and she could hear the sympathy behind his good-humored observation.

"They are," she agreed. Did he understand? She wondered if he realized that she was so reluctant because, despite all her precautions, defenses, and judgments . . . she was starting to really care about Julian Sharpe. She looked back at him, relieved to see a friendly smile on his face.

"Hungry?" he asked.

This time it was she who mentally supplied the innuendo to his innocent remark. Yes, she was hungry for his lips, his arms, his warm, soft skin against hers—she shook the images from her mind. "Starved," she told him.

"Then what are we standing around in the dark talking

for?" he asked, without a trace of irony. "Let's go in."

Pointedly not taking her arm, but politely indicating she should step ahead of him, Julian acted for all the world as if the subject they'd just been discussing was closed for good. As she walked up the back steps, Kelly supposed she should have felt relieved.

Then why was she feeling disappointed?

"All right, you guys!" Annie leaned back in her chair, contentedly licking a spot of whipped cream off her thumb from the homemade pumpkin pie the five of them had just devoured. "If you're all so awesomely magical, let's see you make these dishes disappear."

Julian shot James an amused glance across the table. "That's easy enough, isn't it? Say, Theo—"

"No way." Their assistant shook his curly mane. "I was on KP last night."

"I'll help," Kelly offered, starting to rise. "After a great meal like that, it's the least—"

But James was on his feet, impatiently waving Kelly down. "I will now demonstrate the amazing Sharpe tablecloth maneuver," he announced in an archly sonorous tone. "Never seen before and never duplicated..." He was moving to the head of the heavily laden table, waving his hands with a flourish over the myriad remains of their chicken dinner. As Kelly watched apprehensively, he gripped the edge of the tablecloth in both hands.

"Don't you dare!" Annie shrieked in horror, bolting from her seat.

Kelly looked to Julian, who was stroking his mustache and doing his best to keep a straight face. He caught Kelly's eye and winked.

"Have you no faith in the powers of the great beyond?" James was asking Annie, who was trying to forcibly remove his hands from the tablecloth.

"Not when there's a whole set of dishes involved," she growled. "Would you kindly get your hands—"

"Faithless woman!" he scowled. "Watch, now, as the impossible is made real before your very eyes—"

With a wince of painful apprehension Annie clapped her hands over her eyes, as James made a great show of preparing to yank the cloth. When, a few moments later, there was silence in the room except for Kelly's stifled attempts to keep from giggling, Annie peeked out again.

The table was intact. But as James pompously waved his arms about with an exaggerated flourish, it rose slowly in the air. Kelly's eyes widened in shock. Then she realized that both Julian and Theo, who were seated across from each other, had assumed odd positions, their faces reddening with exertion.

"Very funny," sighed Annie. "But levitating those dishes isn't gonna clean 'em."

"Wrong trick!" James exclaimed, slapping his forehead in mock dismay. "Honey, I'm sorry—I did my best—"

"You did?" Kelly asked. "Then why is your brother the one breaking out in a sweat?" She leaned over, unable to resist tickling Julian in the ribs as he fought to maintain his composure while holding the table up with his knees and hands.

"Whoa!" he yelped, cracking up. The table teetered dangerously, tilting toward them. Quickly Theo lowered his side, and the coffeepot stopped in its progress toward Julian's lap. As the table hit the floor again with a wobbly thud, and silverware clattered to the floor, Annie and Kelly dissolved in laughter. Then the men joined in, James exhorting imaginary spirits to wash the dishes, as womankind were lazy—this last remark resulting in Annie's delivering him a swift kick in the butt—and everyone present was soon shaking in paroxysms of laughter.

Kelly wiped her eyes, then bent to retrieve her fork from the floor, nearly bumping heads with Julian, who was doing the same. As he grinned at her beneath the table, Kelly felt a surge of affection pass between them that had a new flavor to it. Surfacing at the table again, looking around her, she knew what it was.

She was feeling welcome—like family, here on the farm. Though the dinner conversation had veered in and out of "entertainment talk," as Annie termed it, Kelly hadn't had any sense of being excluded. Julian had made it a point to bring her into whatever was being discussed. And with Annie's interest in Kelly's metropolitan life, she'd had her share of being the center of attention. Both James and Annie seemed to accept her, unquestioningly. The wine and good food, and Julian's unusual loquaciousness—he seemed to open up more and relax in his brother's presence—had made Kelly feel completely at ease before long.

"I still don't understand why people pay good money to see a buffoon like you," Annie was telling James in mock disgust as he tried to pull her into his lap when she rose to get more coffee.

"They're really there to see me," Julian said, grinning.

"What's happened to public taste?" Kelly added.

"Down the tubes," James answered.

"Hold onto those leftovers," Julian admonished Kelly, who was clearing her place.

"Right," Theo said, rising. "It's time for Siegfried's snack."

Kelly pitched in to help Annie collect the leftovers for the leopard, and Theo went outside with them. As she washed her hands in the sink, she felt Julian's arm slide around her waist. This time, she stiffened only momentarily, then relaxed, indulging herself in the titillating feeling of his body brushing hers under the pretense of friendly familiarity.

"Enjoy your dinner?" he murmured at her ear.

"Completely," she told him. "I can't remember the last time I've felt so at home with a bunch of people I barely know," she admitted, smiling, then broke from his embrace, facing him with her dripping hands held high. "Got a dish towel handy? Or shall I use this nice black shirt of yours—"

"Jim! Julian! C'mere, guys—quick!"

Julian whirled around as Theo's alarmed voice rang through the back screen door. Both brothers dashed from the kitchen. Annie joined Kelly at the door, worriedly peering into the darkness.

Theo was kneeling at the front of a caged enclosure some yards away from the kitchen. Julian bent over him, examining a piece of leather rein. James was darting about the edges of the barn, making an odd whistling noise with his fingers and mouth.

"Look's like Siegfried's flown the coop," Annie muttered, opening the door. Kelly followed her over to where Julian and Theo knelt.

"Siggy!" James called into the darkness. He whistled again, then disappeared around the barn.

Theo's face was ashen. "I knew this leather would give sooner or later," he said ruefully, with a guilt-stricken look. "Of all the stupid things I ever—"

"Hey, I was the one who said we didn't need the chain when he was home," Julian assured the young man quickly. He put a consoling hand on Theo's shoulder. "There's no need for you to blame yourself. And there's no time now for blaming anybody," he added.

"I guess you're right," Theo said resignedly, straightening up. "There's no telling how long he's been gone— could be ten minutes, or it could be an hour." He looked up at Julian expectantly.

"Look, you take the Jeep over into Stockton County and tell the sheriff, okay?" Julian said. "I don't want any farmer taking a shotgun to Sig because he doesn't know a tame leopard when he sees one."

"Right." Theo nodded, his face brightening. "And I'll tell Mr. Wilson to call some of the locals." He turned, obviously grateful he could do something to redeem himself, and ran off.

"We'll cover the property," Julian called after him. "Don't worry."

Kelly was touched by Julian's paternal behavior. If he was upset with Theo, he'd masked it well. Now, as James joined him in front of the empty pen, the two brothers exchanged a wordless look. Then Julian shook his head with a rueful grin. "If he gets over to the next county, there could be hell to pay."

"You mean, chickens to eat," James chuckled.

"Has this happened before?" Kelly asked.

"Once, when we had a little fire here," Julian told her. "Sig went over toward Lexington and ate up half the state's poultry supply."

"Did anybody get hurt?"

Both men stared at her a moment, then laughed. "A couple of sprained ankles from some scared teenagers perfecting the one-minute mile." Julian grinned. "But Sig wouldn't hurt anybody. We're only concerned that someone who doesn't know better'll try to hurt *him*."

"Well..." James scratched his head thoughtfully. "I guess we've got our evening activity cut out for us."

"You take south and circle eastward," Julian told him. "We'll head north by northwest." He turned to Kelly with a twinkle in his eye. "So, city slicker—did you happen to pack a pair of hiking boots?"

Kelly shook her head. "Just sneakers."

"Hope they're not white," Julian said gravely. "Come on—it's time to scour hill and dale."

She might have known, Kelly reflected, on her way upstairs, that a night in the country wouldn't equal peace and quiet. She'd probably find that back in Manhattan, along with a good night's sleep. Perhaps.

Chapter 6

"IF SOMEONE HAD told me a week ago," Kelly said, as she trudged through the tall grass with Julian in the bright moonlight, "that I would be walking through the wilds of Nebraska tracking a leopard one night..."

"What would you rather be doing?" Julian asked. "Hanging out in some New York City discothèque?"

"I hate discothèques."

"So what would you be doing?"

"Give me a minute and I'll think of something." She stopped behind Julian, who was pausing to pry a piece of rusted barbed wire off an old, broken-down wooden fence that apparently marked the edge of the Sharpe brothers' property. As she watched, he put a foot up, then deftly leaped over the fencing.

"Give me a hand."

"Why?" she joked. "You don't look like you need one."

"Come, Miss Robbins." He sighed, extending his hand.

Kelly stepped up to the fence and, with Julian's assistance, navigated her way over the wire. Her sneakers sank an inch into the loose dirt on the other side, and as she floundered momentarily, Julian steadied her until she'd found her balance.

"Thanks," she murmured, noticing that any time he touched her, her heartbeat quickened automatically. Well, she mused, with an inward sigh, she'd just have to get used to it—as if such nonchalance could ever be possible where this tall, dark, and handsome fellow was concerned.

"Thought of it?"

Kelly looked at him blankly, noting that the moonlight accentuated the rugged lines of his face. "Thought of what?"

"What else you'd rather be doing," he said patiently.

Looking up at him, with the wind riffling his tousled hair, a number of inappropriate replies occurred to her, but she stifled them. "Oh, I don't know—maybe enjoying an aperitif at a nice outdoor café."

"Would you settle for some wine? We are outdoors, after all."

"I suppose," she said. "But where—"

The pop of a cork stopped her in mid-sentence. Julian had produced a bottle of red wine from the little black shoulderbag he carried.

"I thought you said you had a flashlight in there."

"Among other things." He handed her the bottle and watched as she took an experimental sip.

"It's good," she acknowledged, handing it to him. Julian took a healthy swig, then recorked the bottle, starting to walk again.

"And the service is prompt," he said. "No waiting for a table—"

"There are no tables."

"You're wrong again."

He indicated a fallen tree that stretched across their path and, with a leap and a bound, was perched on it, gesturing that she should join him. Smiling, she walked over, and with a show of delicately seating herself, fluffing her skirt primly about her legs, she took the wine bottle from his outstretched hand.

"No noisy crowds," he observed. "No cloud of cigarette smoke, no check or tipping involved..."

"You're absolutely right," she said as her second swallow of wine billowed like a warm, velvety cloud inside of her. "There's no place I would rather be."

"A canopy of stars," he went on, indicating the sky, which was indeed filled with more starlight than she'd ever seen back East. "Cool breezes and a full moon..."

"And a tame but nonetheless running-wild beast," she reminded him. "Shouldn't we keep moving? You don't seem particularly concerned."

"I'm sure we'll find him soon enough," he said, taking

the bottle from her. "Or James and Annie will. Siegfried's not likely to go across the highway, and that's just a mile or so from here—spans the edge of the next farm's property in a half circle." He pointed in an arc ahead of them, where a glade of trees rustled in the soft wind. "At this time of night I don't think he'd come across many unsuspecting natives."

"Then I'm willing to sit for a bit," she said.

"Winded already?"

"Not at all," she protested. "I'm just admiring the view."

"Fine with me," he said, handing her the bottle. "I'll just admire you. I know the view backward and forward."

"Are you compulsively flirtatious?" she asked him. "Or have you just been in show business too long?"

"Oh, that's right—I'm Mr. Insincerity," he said breezily. "But actually, Kelly, I'm capable of meaning a compliment. You should know me better."

"No, I shouldn't," she said, after a long sip of wine, then giggled. "Sorry. I mean, I don't. Know you."

He was looking at her in an oddly serious way, and the soft glow of aroused interest in his eyes held her, pulling her in, undercutting her light, bantering mood.

"You could get to know me," he said softly.

"I'm not sure it's so easy," she said, turning away to watch a pair of fireflies dart and spark in the air. She was reluctant to begin a deeper conversation. "You're the secretive one, remember?"

"You make me feel like telling secrets," he said, and there was a gruffness in his tone that made her realize he was unaccustomed to being this candid with a... what? she wondered. A non-conquest?

"Then tell me one," she said, meeting his eyes again.

"Any one?"

"You pick," she said.

He looked at her, and in the clarity of moonlight she could see his inward debate. She sensed him measuring one reply against the other, and watching a parade of subtle expressions flit across his handsome face, she was filled with an urge to reach out and stroke the soft, tanned skin of his cheek. She suppressed it.

"I sing in the shower," he said at length.

Kelly laughed. "That's your idea of a secret?"

"You've never heard me sing," he said gravely. "It might destroy whatever image of me you have."

"I don't have one image of you," she blurted out impulsively. "Your image keeps changing."

He cocked his head. "Changing into what?" he asked, smiling.

"It's hard to say." She avoided the issue, taking the wine bottle from him and having another quick sip. Make that the last, she warned herself. She could feel herself drifting into a convivially uninhibited state that was not at all conducive to maintaining... What was she supposed to be maintaining? Oh, yes—professional distance. "But you haven't told me a *real* secret," she chided him. "Something more personal." She handed the wine bottle back.

This time he didn't hesitate, so the honest seriousness of his response took her by surprise. "I've never really been... friends with a woman," he said quietly, holding the bottle, not drinking.

"You mean..." Her mind teetered between teasing and talking, really talking. "You mean, like we are? Friends?"

"It seems that's what we are," he allowed.

"That's a sweet thing to say," she told him, instinctively putting her hand on his knee, then awkwardly removing it. She cleared her throat. "But, go on, Julian. Explain. Haven't you ever been more deeply involved than—"

"And I can't say I like it much," he interrupted. She sensed some real resentment in his voice. "What I mean to say is," he went on, in a more subdued tone, "I'm not used to being forced into a... purely platonic relationship with a woman that I'm so—"

A sudden rustling noise in the woods ahead of them brought Julian to his feet in mid-sentence. Kelly started to speak but he shushed her with his hand, listening intently. Then he cupped his mouth and made the same distinctive whistle his brother had made earlier. As they both watched, the tiny figure of what looked like a rabbit scurried quickly

Under His Spell

from under a thicket and then disappeared behind a tree. Julian shook his head, and then resolutely popped the cork back into the bottle.

"Let's get going," he said, helping her off the tree trunk.

His pace seemed quicker to Kelly now as she fell in step with him—or was the wine slowing her down? She couldn't help but feel that Julian had been glad for the interruption. But she'd caught another glimmer of sensitivity showing through the cracks in his carefully composed manner, and this only served to pique her interest.

"You were saying?"

Julian pulled a branch aside to allow her passage. They were entering the thick of the little woods, and the moonlight didn't penetrate as easily. He whistled again, into the darkness, listened, then walked on.

"I forget," he said casually as their feet crackled on the little needles and leaves. "I think the wine was talking."

"Oh." Could she leave it at that? Maybe it was best. For the moment she was content to walk, more slowly, at his side, staring wide-eyed at the silver moonbeams dappling swaying branches all around them. On a night like this, she could almost imagine a forest could be enchanted.

"Smell that evergreen?"

She nodded. "It's heavenly." A bird chirped and another answered so close she nearly jumped. Julian chuckled softly.

"Don't tell me you're still spooked."

"No." She laughed. "There aren't any ghosts here, are there? Or wild animals?"

"Possibly some elves," he joked. "But the only wild animal within miles should answer when called." He cupped his mouth and whistled again. There was no answering roar. But Kelly suddenly noticed a faint rustling sound that came from up ahead.

"Is that . . . water?"

Julian nodded. "There's a stream that runs through here. We'll go around it to where there's rocks big enough to cross."

She followed him as he wended his way through the trees. There was no real path, but he seemed to be following a trail he was familiar with. Kelly watched the moonlight illuminate his solid frame, then lose it, as he walked ahead. The moon was getting to her. Or the sweet forest air. Try as she could, all she could think about was wanting the embrace she'd spurned just hours before. And he? Had he really put all such thoughts behind?

They were approaching the stream now. Its gentle churning was louder, and she could glimpse a sparkle of silvery water through the foliage. Julian had gotten farther ahead of her, and he paused to let her catch up. She ducked to miss a branch, but a leaf caught in her hair. Julian deftly plucked it out. She looked at his face, shadowy, unfathomable. What was he thinking?

"Wine?" He uncorked the bottle again.

Kelly shrugged. She was thirsty, after all. The tangy, cool liquid was delicious, and she took another gulp, heedless of whatever its effects might be. The night and the gentle warmth of Julian's fingers as he took the bottle from her, his hand over hers, were undermining all her rational thoughts, bewitching her with the heady forest scents and the nearness of him.

"Sig?" Julian called. "Siegfried?"

Impulsively, Kelly took up the cry. "Siegfried!" she called. "Siggy!"

Julian laughed, and then they both chimed in together, calling the leopard through the forest glade's dim echo and rush of water. "Show me how you whistle," she urged him.

Julian demonstrated. She attempted the whistle, but all that came out was a useless sputter. Chuckling, Julian showed her again, cupping his hands to her face to help. Still, she couldn't master it, and laughing, she backed away from him, then stumbled onward, unable to stop her momentum. They were in a gradual slope that led down to the river, and she found herself running now, with Julian close behind, through the tall grass and bushes to the river sparkling beyond.

When they stood on the bank, breathless, he wordlessly pointed to the large craggy rocks off to their left, where crossing looked easiest. Nodding, Kelly followed him. She

Under His Spell 109

was on the first of the rocks, close behind Julian, when a little splash distracted her and she leaned over to get a better look below.

"Julian!" she said, delighted. "There's fish!"

"Of course there's fish," he said, amused. "Is it all coming back to you now? Your carefree childhood in the wilds of New England?"

"It is," she said, and leaned recklessly closer to the water, only a foot or so beneath the rock. "How deep is it? Is it—"

She was slipping before she could stop herself. With a yelp, she lost her balance on the rock. Waving her arms frantically, she caught her balance—barely—as she landed in the water, miraculously still upright.

"Did you find out how deep it is?" he asked.

"Funny," she muttered, taking an experimental step. "I could have broken my neck."

"And all for the love of fish?" He shook his head. "Well, you might as well wade on. I'll meet you on the other side."

"Thanks," she said. "It doesn't get any deeper?"

"No." His eyes were drifting to her bare thighs, revealed as she lifted the soaked bottom of her skirt. "Quite a provocative picture," he murmured. "Lady of the lake..."

"That's not a very platonic look in your eyes," Kelly said. "Do you mind—"

Grumbling something under his breath, Julian looked away. The stream's bottom was relatively flat, though her sneakers were soon sinking in the mud. With each step she seemed to sink a little farther in. Fortunately the other bank was just a few more strides.

"Need any help?" He was already at the bank's edge.

"No, thank you," she said, with as much dignity as she could muster. The water was soothingly cool on her bare legs, and if it wasn't for the muck around her socks, she wouldn't have minded this semi-dip. Grabbing onto some long reeds hanging over the water, she struggled to pull herself out. But the pull of the bottom threw her off. As she lifted herself up, her sneaker caught, her ankle turned— and she fell backward with a startled shriek.

Julian grabbed hold of her arm. She rocked forward into him, nearly pulling him into the water with her. But he stood firm. As she clung to him, he hoisted her up into the air. Suddenly aloft, a prisoner in his arms, she lost her breath, her heart pounding.

He lifted her easily above the water, over the tufts of reeds, and then slowly lowered her down onto a grassy bank filled with pillows of Scottish moss. As she felt the earth beneath her, she realized, dimly, that her soaked skirt was bunched above her thighs, that his arm was still around her. Julian was bending over her, cradling her to him in the darkness, shafts of moonlight making his eyes seem to glint wildly as she gazed up at him, breathless.

"You fool," he murmured. "You damned fool."

"It could have happened to anyone," she began weakly. "I lost my—"

"I'm not talking about that," he said, his voice smoldering with an intensity just barely held in check. "I'm talking about us. Why have you insisted on us playing this childish game?"

"Game? What—"

"I can't be only friends with you," he said in a husky growl. "I can't be casual when I care about you the way I do. I've wanted you ever since I first laid eyes on you; you know that!"

Her fingers were splayed against his chest as he leaned in closer, his face only inches from hers, his eyes alight with undisguised desire. His hard masculine frame, melded so close to her soft curves, set her trembling skin aflame.

"No," she whispered. "I only thought..."

"You think too much," he murmured hoarsely. "You'll think of any excuse to keep me from doing the only thing I want to do—which is to hold you in my arms like this— to kiss you—"

His fingers tangled in her hair, tilting her head backward as his mouth covered hers, coaxing her lips apart with a burning urgency that sent a shiver running through her from head to toe. The passion she'd been trying to deny within herself rose and instinctively she fitted her body to his as

Under His Spell

their kiss deepened. Arching her hips against his taut body, she could feel the potent maleness of him stiffening in response. His hungry lips pressed harder, the sweet savagery of their kiss melting any remnants of resistance away. Her arms slid round his shoulders as his hands curved around her buttocks, pressing her closer.

"Kelly..." he breathed, his lips leaving hers with a panting whisper. "You can't tell me you don't want this for us." His eyes were almost closed, a gleaming fire glinting from beneath his long, dark lashes. "Why are you always trying to pull away?"

"Because..." she breathed hoarsely. "It wouldn't mean a thing to you. I'm not naïve. I know—"

"You don't know," he said, eyes flashing. "I've fallen for you, damn it—whether you like it or not. I'm not so sure *I* like it—thinking about you, day and night, hardly being able to keep my eyes on the road when you're sitting so close..."

With a growl of desire, he kissed her again, his warm moist lips darting from her lips to her cheek, the hollow of her neck, and back again in a brief frenzy of affection. Every touch of him inflamed her anew, and she squirmed languidly in his powerful grip, a soft moan escaping from her lips.

"You're crazy," she whispered, her breath quickening as the flattened mounds of her breasts heaved upward to touch his chest and then receded. The powerful pressure of his body against hers was driving her mad with arousal, and even as she spoke she knew all protest was meaningless. "You can't be serious. This is only..."

"Only what?" he whispered. "I know illusions when I see them, Kelly, but this is real. The feeling I have for you is real. You can't fight it off yourself... I can see it in your eyes."

Weak beneath his penetrating gaze, mind hazy with reeling arousal as her body came to life beneath his searching caresses, she took one long, shuddering breath. "What... do you see?"

"Love," he whispered huskily. "Love..."

And then his mouth plundered hers once more and her own desire ignited against his parted lips. Long-repressed yearnings surged to life in his embrace. Falling back against the soft and pliant moss, she pulled him to her.

A heated rush of arousal poured through her as his hands slid up the damp fabric of her blouse to cup her breasts, kneading the soft mounds with his strong, smooth palms. A sigh of unrestrained pleasure came from deep in her throat. "You're right," she whispered. "I can't fight you anymore..."

"Trust me," he whispered, his lips sliding across her cheek to gently nibble at her ear. "Let go..."

The smoldering insistence of his husky voice sent a tremor to the core of her. Something within her gave way. Wordlessly she brought her lips to meet his, her arms tightening around him, legs unstiffening, her body silently signaling her surrender.

This time their kiss was slower, sweeter. He seemed to savor the taste of her as she savored him. Her last rebellion gone, she twisted beneath him only to fit closer to his lean, muscular lines. With a muffled groan of desire, he sank his lips into the hollow of her neck, kissing and nibbling a searing path to the top of her breasts, his fingers swiftly and deftly undoing the buttons of her blouse.

His hand tightened on the firm softness of one breast, revealed now in the pale moonlight, and he bent his mouth to tease and lick the stiffening tip, eliciting a strangled moan of pleasure from her. Then he nibbled tenderly on the other and she arched her back, a simmering glow of arousal spreading from his languidly probing mouth and hands.

Deliberately now, she moved against him, sliding her legs up alongside his, glorying in the feel of the power she aroused beneath his hips. With a sigh of satisfaction, Julian reached under the soaked linen of her skirt, tightening his grip on her firm, soft buttocks. Then he gathered the material, and in one movement eased it down past her waist. She let herself fall back and he glided the skirt down her legs.

Under His Spell

She lay before him, nearly naked, her breasts rising and falling in the softly luminous light. He looked down at her, his eyes running possessively over her, resting briefly on the supple curves of her hip beneath her sheer panties, then traveling to her naked thighs, a smile of anticipation turning to amusement as his gaze fell on her feet.

"You're a Venus in wet sneakers," he murmured with a throaty chuckle. "No, don't move," he cautioned her as she sat up. He knelt at her feet and quickly untied the soggy laces, removing the sneakers, covered with mud, and then the equally mired socks. As she watched, he stretched out, leaning over the bank of the stream, and washed his hands in the rushing clean waters. Then he was back, hovering over her, sprinkling her nakedness with drops of silvery water. She gasped, shivering, but loving the feel of it; loving even more the soft wetness of his hands as he ran them slowly over her body.

"I love your hands," she breathed. "They're so beautifully shaped..."

"And my fingers love the feel of your beautiful shape," he murmured. He bent to kiss the soft roundness of her belly, then slowly slid the elastic band of her panties down, his lips following in the wake of the sheer material. She shuddered as he lightly kissed and licked the velvet softness of her inner thighs, then traced a path down one trembling leg.

He paused again, his eyes drinking in her total nudity, and began to unbutton his own shirt. "Allow me," she whispered.

She sat up, unbuttoning his shirt quickly, and slipping it off his shoulders. She trailed her fingers eagerly over the dark down on his chest, leaning forward to gently kiss his small male nipples until they were as erect with arousal as her own. Then she slid her hand down the flat contours of his stomach, feeling his muscles tighten at her touch.

Then she undid his belt, slowly slid his trousers' zipper down, and with a little shiver of anticipation, slipped her hands beneath the band of his undershorts, sliding pants and shorts down his legs to reveal the powerful manhood that had strained against the cloth.

When he was as fully naked as she, he lay beside her on the soft bank of moss, his glittering eyes devouring her body as she admired his. His trim musculature seemed as polished as sculpted marble in the white moonlight, which accentuated the supple lines of his arms, shoulders, and thighs.

Then with tender passion they began, at last, a deliciously slow dance of love in the soft grass. His strong, powerful hands explored her every curve, as she explored his. His touch was alternately soft and fierce, demanding and giving.

Bracing himself on his elbows, he ran his tongue around each pliant breast, circling the rosy centers until she trembled with pleasure. With slow, leisurely kisses and nibbles, he caressed and licked his way down her taut stomach, his fingers deftly playing with the tangled blond velvet tuft at the juncture of her thighs.

A deepening ache of warm desire began to pulsate from deep within her as his fingers gently grazed and teased the tender flesh that throbbed hotly for his touch. She began to writhe slowly beneath him as his lips replaced his hands, and he planted moist warm kisses over her soft belly, inching himself lower, leaving her poised with aching, nervous expectancy on the brink, teasing her with his tongue and lips, until she moaned his name, twisting underneath him in exquisite torment.

Just when she could barely stand it, he shifted his weight again, pressing himself against her and covering her mouth with his urgent lips. His hands continued to touch her, intimately, till her breathing was raspy and shallow. She gripped the carved muscles of his hips, pulling him closer, her hands squeezing and kneading his supple loins and buttocks, until his breath was as shuddery and hoarse as hers.

And then he was poised above her and she wrapped herself around him, parting her thighs to accept him with a joyful cry as he surged forward, seeking and then crossing the final threshold. He slowed then, softly calling her name, until she opened her eyes, meeting his.

Their eyes locked as he slowly thrust into the deepest heart of her, and he held her gaze as she clung to him, reveling in his controlled power, hungering for each thrust as they rose together to a higher and higher plateau of pleasure.

Soon they were moving faster, and she was breathless with every spiraling peak, digging her fingers into his tensing muscles. Still he held her eyes, watching the passion flame and burn brighter, until at last, with a groan of unleashed desire, he pulled her even tighter and they soared together even higher, the fires that burned within them bursting, cresting into a united spire of white-hot flame.

It seemed that the rushing sound of the stream filled her ears as she swooned, bathed in sweat, holding him tightly to her, savoring the last slow undulations of passion. The moon swam into focus above her, beyond the darkened silhouette of her lover, and she could feel the soft wet moss pillowing her head, where before she had felt only his embrace. Softly, Julian kissed her forehead, then tenderly pulled a strand of hair from her mouth.

"Sweetheart," he said huskily, "I only wish you could see yourself as I'm seeing you now... with your hair all wild, your face flushed, your lips still wet with lovemaking..."

He kissed her again. "You mean I'm a mess," she whispered weakly. "No, don't—" She gasped instinctively as he shifted his weight.

Julian stayed within her, smiling. "The most beautiful mess I've ever seen," he said. "You don't want me to go now?"

She shook her head, feeling wanton, free, and uninhibited beneath his frankly lustful gaze. "I know we should," she whispered. "But you feel so good..."

"You're right." He smiled. "I feel unbelievably good."

Kelly laughed. As his laughter joined hers she felt it reverberate through her body as they lay skin to skin, a deliciously erotic sensation. "I love to hear you laugh," she whispered. "And feel it, too... Oh, Julian," she sighed, as he bent to kiss her neck once more. "I'll tell you a secret now."

He looked at her expectantly. "*You* sing in the shower, too?"

"Serious secret," she said. "I've never done this before."

"Kelly Robbins." He frowned. "You can't expect me to believe you're a—"

"No, silly—I mean I've never... made love in a forest at night," she said softly. "Julian Sharpe—you really *are* a magician. You have the most extraordinary power to... make me go absolutely wild, I guess."

"No." He shook his head, tenderly tracing the outline of her lips with his fingers. "It's you. I look into your eyes and I see the wildness there. I see a dare..."

"A dare?"

He nodded. "You're daring me to bring it out... to come out of myself, and meet you halfway."

"Umm," she murmured. She slid out her tongue to lick his finger playfully. "You know," she reflected, "I like you better like this."

"Like what?"

"Open," she said simply. "Unguarded... not so mysterious."

"And you," he replied. "I like you better when you're not fighting me off."

"I've had my reasons," she murmured.

"I'd like to know them."

"Now?" she protested, and she drew a shudder of contentment from him as she wrapped her legs even tighter around his hips.

"A little later," he agreed. "Now's the time we should forget reason altogether..." he whispered. "Now..."

She raised an eyebrow. "Now?" But as he moved against her, teasing her nipples into quivering arousal again with the tickling curls of his chest hair, she could feel that his arousal was undiminished. Closing her eyes, she stretched slowly in his arms, arching her back, delighting in the feel of him, his body responding to her every move.

As he nuzzled her neck with his lips and tongue, she

Under His Spell 117

nearly purred like a contented cat. In fact, she was purring... or, rather—

Kelly's eyes flew open. "Julian," she breathed. "We're not alone."

Julian lifted his head, startled. "Who—"

Then his gaze followed hers to the other side of the riverbank, where Siegfried sat, head cradled in his paws, eyes open in obvious interest at the show across the way, a steady rumble coming from his throat. As they stared at him, the leopard lifted his head and shook it in a nodding motion, then settled back again, as if bidding them to continue.

"If I didn't know better," Kelly began, feeling a giggle starting up inside of her, "I'd think he was encouraging us."

"Don't kid yourself." Julian grinned. "As one animal to another, I'm sure he approves."

As she walked across the open meadows, arm in arm with Julian under the starry sky, Kelly felt like a character from *Midsummer Night's Dream*. She was clad only in her oversized blouse, which fell to mid-thigh, and Julian had fashioned a little wreath of purple wildflowers for her hair. The ground was moist and soft beneath her bare feet—he had packed her soaked sneakers, socks, and skirt in his bag—and with the leopard trotting leisurely ahead of them toward the farm, and the taste of the last dregs of wine still fresh in her mouth, her body still tingling with the feel of Julian's, she felt she was indeed in a dream.

Without even thinking, she began to hum a little melody, not sure what. Julian joined in after a few bars, acutely off key, and she stopped, laughing.

"You don't even know what song it was!" she said.

"'I Feel Pretty,'" he told her. "An appropriate tune. You do, you know." He ran his hand through her hair affectionately.

"I feel wild," she admitted, breaking away from him, skipping ahead a few steps. "To tell you the truth, it feels strange to be wearing clothes on a night like this." She twirled around, watching the stars circle above her.

Julian chuckled behind her. "Another side to Kelly Robbins," he joked. "Is this the way you are when you're happy?"

"Am I happy?" she considered. "Possibly," she teased him. As he tried to grab hold of her, she darted away again. "Hey!" she called. "Is this the famous Sharpe effect—the one that makes you feel like you're floating?"

"Could be." He smiled. "Are your feet off the ground?"

"Actually, no," she said. "They're in the cool grass."

He caught hold of her again, his eyes glinting with mischief. "Let's get you higher," he said.

"More wine?" She widened her eyes at him in comic dismay. "Then I'd really float home."

"No, a different kind of lift." He whistled. "Sig! Over here."

The leopard stopped in its stride, looked back over its shoulder, then sauntered up to Julian. His master bade him to sit, and then, as Kelly protested, laughing, he lifted her up, putting her astride the leopard's back. He gave the beast another command, and suddenly Kelly found herself borne aloft on Siegfried.

"Oh, no!" she cried helplessly. "I'm too heavy—what if he gets annoyed or something—"

"You're doing fine," he called, grinning. "Just hold on to his neck. It's only another minute's walk to the farm."

The leopard seemed nearly oblivious to his load, and Kelly settled into her furry perch with an amused shrug. The lights from the farm glimmered across the expanse of field ahead of her. Siegfried padded slowly onward, as Julian walked beside them, vastly amused.

When they reached the back porch in this fashion, James and Annie were there to greet them. Kelly suddenly felt acutely self-conscious and blushed as Julian helped her down, to the other couple's applause. She felt as if her glow from wine and lovemaking was as obvious as neon.

"You must've followed him clear over into the Dakotas," James drawled, as he led Siegfried over to his newly installed chain.

"He found us, actually," said Julian. Kelly met his glance and looked away, afraid her blush was deepening. Annie was looking at her with a shrewdly knowing expression on her face.

"Beautiful night for leopard chasing," she said casually, following Kelly into the house. "Seems to have done you a world of good."

Kelly could only murmur her assent. Embarrassed, she quickly made her way upstairs, determined to throw some cold water on her face and try to regain her scattered senses.

The soft knock on her bedroom door sometime later, when the household had ostensibly settled down to bed, didn't surprise her. It would have been sheer self-deception to think she hadn't been expecting it—no, waiting for it—as she brushed her hair in the cozy little eaved room. Kelly put down her brush and went softly to the door.

Julian peered through the crack as she held it open. "Hello," he said softly.

"Hi," she said, feeling a smile creep onto her lips before she could stop it.

"Well, aren't you going to invite me in?"

"Oh," she said. "Is there something..."

"Kelly Robbins," he said, his eyes narrowing. "Open this door."

"Brute," she muttered, and ushered him inside, closing the door after him. He seemed to loom even larger in the low-ceilinged room. Kelly stood near the door, self-consciously holding her robe closed. She was aware of her nakedness beneath the flimsy terry cloth, and the way his eyes caressed her in the soft light of the lamp by the bed showed he was aware of it as well.

"How are you?" he asked quietly.

"Fine," she said.

"Are you sure?" He took a step closer. "I noticed that once we were back in the house you avoided me. In fact, for the past hour you've been trying to act like nothing at all had happened between us."

"Well, I..." Kelly stopped, biting her lip. He was right, of course. Ever since she'd come inside, regrets and self-recriminations had been seeping into her befuddled brain.

She'd been a fool. She'd lost her head. She'd violated every conceivable rule of behavior she'd fashioned for herself—and what really worried her was, she'd loved it.

"I've got this funny idea," he said slowly, "that you still don't trust me."

"I'm not used to trusting men," she said, looking away from his searching gaze.

He stepped closer and lifted her chin with his hand, forcing her, firmly but gently, to look him in the eye. "I'm not just men," he said mildly. "I'm *me*. And I told you I'd fallen in love with you. You think it was only a line?"

"I..." His direct gaze, the gleaming power of his eyes' velvet depths, coaxed the answer from her before she had time to think. "I don't know what to think. I'm starting to care about you, care for you—and—"

"And?" His fingers gently traced the line of her cheek.

"And it scares me!" she blurted out.

"I know," he said simply. "The concept shakes me up a bit."

"You mean you're worried? That I'll—I'll try to tie you down, or something? You're afraid of hurting my feelings?"

In answer, he grabbed her by the arms and forcibly pulled her over to the bed, sitting her down so abruptly it took her breath away. "Now, look," he said, anger glinting in his eyes as he sat down beside her, still holding onto her arms. "You've got to stop that stuff. I'm trying to tell you we're in this together, and you keep talking to me as if I was somebody else! I don't know who the guy was who made you this suspicious, but Kelly..."—he loosened his grip, his gaze softening at the hurt look he saw in her face—"...I'm not him."

"You're a lot like him," she said, swallowing as her throat tightened with emotion. "He was an entertainer, like you. Like you, he was always on the road. And I don't mean to—to offend you, Julian, but I haven't met a traveling entertainer yet, in my years at *Omnibus*, who wasn't some kind of flirtatious philanderer. You people don't have the time or the inclination to settle down and get serious about someone—"

Under His Spell

"Kelly, Kelly..." He stroked her hair gently, shaking his head in rueful sympathy. "You've been burned good and deep, haven't you?"

She sighed, fighting the feelings welling up inside her. "You could say that," she muttered. "And I'm not about to let it happen again."

He was silent a moment. Then his hand dropped to grasp her shoulder lightly. "Listen," he said quietly, "what you say may be true of some. But believe me when I tell you—I've had just about enough of the road, and the kind of meaningless encounters that go with it—mine, by the way, have been few and far between, no matter what you might think. Look at me," he commanded softly. Kelly swallowed and met his gaze. "Are you believing me?"

Kelly bit her lower lip. "I'd like to," she murmured.

"Maybe I've been searching," he went on, the soft glow in his dark eyes holding her gaze, "for something more—something worth giving up things for..." His grasp tightened on her shoulder. "I'm serious about that book I mentioned. I'm ready to stop touring, taking the time off to write it... And now that I've met you—" He smiled. "Don't you feel... changed, somehow?"

"It's true, I guess," she mumbled. "I've been spending a lot of time keeping myself straight, busy, blindered... Then I run into some whacko like you, and..." She shook her head.

"And?"

"And I end up traipsing around the countryside drunk on wine and lust, riding leopards in the moonlight," she sighed. "Too much fun. I'm afraid I'm losing it."

"But you're not losing anything," he said softly, pulling her back with him onto the bed. "My sweet, sweet lady... you could be gaining much more than you ever had before..."

"Conceited fellow, aren't you?" she muttered.

With a grimace of insulted annoyance, he pulled her on top of him and, pinning her arms at her sides, kissed her full on the lips, hungrily plundering the sweet treasure of her mouth. Resistant at first, she soon answered his passion with an urgency of her own, sliding her body to fit against his, the supple musculature of his frame already feeling familiar to her.

"Julian," she moaned, coming up for air, "this isn't getting us anywhere."

"No?" He seemed genuinely surprised. "What I've been trying to tell you is, I am serious about you. I'm not running away, or taking anything for granted. Having you in my arms like this is all I've ever wanted since we met. Why on earth would I want to throw it all away?"

"Keep talking," she said dreamily, as his hands nudged the opening robe from her shoulders. "I'd like to believe you so much..."

His robe was loosening beneath her. Unable to contain herself, she ran her fingers through his curly hair, reveling in the feel of his maleness awakening against her naked thighs as she straddled him.

"You're the kind of woman..." he breathed, stiffening at her caresses.

"Yes?" She shook the robe free from her shoulders, impatiently lifting her arms to allow him to slip it from her.

"The kind of woman who..."

Losing all restraint, she was kissing a line of light wet kisses down his chest now, suddenly the aggressor. A part of her was wondering at her actions. But it was useless to be rational. Julian made her want to lose herself completely, when he touched her. The feel of his naked skin on hers was like an aphrodisiac.

"What kind of woman?"

"The kind..." His breath was coming quicker as she continued onward, running her lips over his lower belly, savoring the taste of him with eager lips.

Suddenly it was he who took command. Rolling over, he pinned her beneath him, gazing at her with smoldering eyes as she waited, taut and breathless, for his lips to claim hers again.

"You're the kind of woman who could change a man's mind," he said, with fierce conviction. "For all you know..."

"Yes?" she breathed, and, unable to restrain herself, lifted her head to kiss him as he gazed at her.

Under His Spell

"For all you know," he went on huskily, "I've been looking for a woman who would ask it all—everything—of me. I've been waiting for a woman like you."

With a growl, he bent to taste her parted lips again. "Oooh," she murmured, as he kissed her neck, nibbling at her ear. "And I've been waiting," she breathed. "To feel like a woman..."

Her slow undulations beneath him drew a groan from deep in his throat. He pressed his lips to hers again, lowering the full length of his body down, adjusting his hips between her opening thighs.

"Feel it," he whispered. "Feel it all—with me..."

She clung to him, exquisite tremors of pleasure coursing through her as they began to move together on the bed. Passion engulfed them in a heady, reeling paroxysm of spiraling desire.

Long into the night they loved, seeking and sharing the most intimate moments. Kelly felt loved as she had never been loved, in Julian's arms. Together they filled the night with pleasure, playful and deeply felt, slowly, quickly, luxuriating in the newness, the discovery of each other.

The sky was graying with the coming dawn, when, spent at last, they drifted into sleep, entwined in each other's arms.

Chapter 7

SUNLIGHT ON HER face woke Kelly some hours later. Instinctively, she felt for the warm body that had been wrapped around her in the dark, but Julian was gone from the bed. Bleary-eyed, she sat up, feeling a delicious exhaustion in every limb.

Yawning, she looked around her. The bedclothes were tangled about the foot of the bed. Even as she shook the sleep from her eyes she still felt woozy with sensual fulfillment. It seemed she'd slept only a moment. As a warm breeze riffled the lace curtains around her window, Kelly stretched, arching her back, then slid her feet to the floor.

Two birds stood chirping on the sill outside. Amused, she watched them, querulously cocking their heads at each other and ruffling their feathers. They stood close by each other and turned at the same instant to face the sky. Then one bent to straighten the other's neck feathers, in what seemed like an affectionate gesture. The other emitted a friendly chirp, and then they were aloft, off again into the wild blue.

Smiling, Kelly thought of her hours in Julian's arms, and how much closer they'd become, with barriers down. She remembered whispered endearments, and lazy, playful conversations about likes and dislikes, hopes for the future, funny stories of the past.

Toward dawn, when it seemed that they couldn't possibly have made love again, she'd massaged Julian's shoulders and he'd told her of his thoughts for the future. He was serious about writing that book on magical hoaxes, he confided—though he wasn't sure about his journalistic skills. Half seriously, she'd offered to help, and he'd seemed genuinely pleased and interested. Then, somehow, the conversation had veered off to other things, as her hands had traveled south of his shoulders, and before long she and Julian had begun yet another reprise of passion...

Kelly rose from the bed, stretching again. The appetite Julian had raised in her for liberated, glorious sexual adventure nearly shocked her when she thought about it. But now a more pragmatic appetite was making its presence known with loud stomach rumblings. Kelly found her discarded robe by the bed and put it on, following the scent of fresh-brewed coffee to the door.

She walked slowly down the hall in her bare feet, yawning again as she rounded the first landing of the stairs. Country music was wafting up from the living room, and a delicious scent of eggs and bacon filtered from the kitchen. She could hear voices in the kitchen as she approached it— Julian and James, she realized.

The front door was open, and she couldn't resist lingering by the screen to savor the view of open countryside a moment. Annie was out in the front yard, tending the little garden of peppers, squash, and other vegetables, while Siegfried sat nearby, tail slowly swaying, his eyes on a flock of blackbirds in a lemon tree. The distant whir of machinery told her Theo was busy in the barn again.

The sweet clean air and sunshine lent the scene an especially appealing glow. She could get used to this atmosphere, she decided—at least in stretches of time. She'd been so determined to acclimate herself to city life, to "grow up" fast, that she'd taken the simple pleasures of a rural life-style for granted. But after so many years in Manhattan, it looked good to her now.

With a small contented sigh, she turned from the door. But as she took a step toward the kitchen, the words she heard through the open doorway slowed her.

"Brussels," James was saying. "Amsterdam looks good. We've got the dates in Paris solid already, but there's also a possibility of going farther north, if you want."

"North?" Julian's voice sounded interested. "You mean they've heard of us in Sweden?"

James chuckled. "Yup, you bet. But Copenhagen is actually the nicest venue. You know, the Koben Haus—"

"Still standing?" Julian's wry chuckle sent a shiver down her spine. Kelly paused outside the doorway, knowing she shouldn't be eavesdropping, but unable to stop herself. What she was hearing was making her heart thump. A European tour? But Julian had said—

"They've rebuilt it since we were there in '80," James went on. "And there's three whole weeks of open time available in early September."

"Sounds good," said Julian. "Why don't you put together a possible itinerary with Mark? I'll look it over when I get back."

"We should move on this pretty quick," said James. "It's already a little late for some of the places—"

"Don't worry," Julian said. "I'm sure we can make a definite decision after this week. I just want to check out the logistics of the whole thing first before jumping ahead. Okay?"

"If you must," James sighed. "But you know Mark—"

"Managers are impatient by nature. I'll call him as soon as I'm back."

Kelly remained stock-still outside the kitchen. That Julian should be planning another tour—when only last night he'd spoken so seriously of taking a long hiatus from the road—was bad enough. But his constant use of the word *I* where she longed to hear a *we* was what really stung her to the quick. He spoke as if she didn't exist, she thought, with growing bitterness.

The brothers' conversation was already turning to more mundane matters: the care and feeding of Siegfried. Julian was leaving the leopard with James while he went on to Colorado and California. Kelly tried to pull her overabundance of emotions together before entering the kitchen.

Had he been handing her a line all along, then? All these veiled and direct references to changing his life-style, to staying in one place—all these declarations of love for her—was it all just a calculated way to wear down her defenses, and make another conquest?

Under His Spell 127

Her hunger was turning to queasiness. And you said you weren't naïve, she told herself angrily. What made you think that a night of love would change anything? You should have known better. You've known the man less than a week and already you're putting your heart right out on the chopping block...

Kelly closed her eyes a moment, trying to stay calm. Then she resolutely belted her robe tighter, then strode into the kitchen.

Julian looked up as she entered with an affectionate smile. "Ah, the sleeping beauty wakes," he joked, and before she could move past him, he halted her with a hug.

His easy affection was difficult to bear just then. She gave him a wan smile and moved on, ostensibly interested in the eggs still steaming on the stove.

"Help yourself, Kelly," James said. "Annie just cooked those up."

"I'll get you a plate," Julian added, rising.

"I'm going to see if Theo's gotten himself electrocuted yet," James said with a grin. "Catch you later."

When his brother had left the kitchen, Julian came up behind Kelly, pulling her gently to him as he put a plate and cup down on the counter next to the stove.

His body against hers reawakened the sensual pulse that always rose when he touched her. It was difficult to think clearly when he turned her around to face him. "Good morning," he said softly, kissing her gently on the lips.

He obviously sensed her lack of response, for he looked at her strangely. "Something wrong?"

Kelly shook her head and turned around again to scoop some eggs from the pan onto her plate. "I hope I didn't interrupt you two," she said carefully.

"You're an interruption I'll always welcome," he said, smiling, and leaned past her to pour some coffee into her cup. "Milk?"

"Please," she muttered, thinking that his choice of words was oddly revealing. Behind the seemingly affectionate phrase, she heard another meaning—that she *was* an interruption, in the regular ebb and flow of his professional life.

As she sat down at the table, purposely avoiding a direct confrontation with his eyes, she wondered how she was supposed to act. Telling him she knew about the upcoming tour would be an open admission of eavesdropping, but something else kept her silent, holding her back from asking him to explain himself.

He should tell her. If he was willing to volunteer information about his plans, to confide in her, then maybe she could suspend judgment—maybe she could begin to trust him again, if he'd just be straight with her. Watching his lean body, clad in tight jeans and the ubiquitous black shirt, move around the table gave a tug to her insides. She'd wanted so much to believe in him, to think that what had passed between them wasn't only a passing fancy...

"Did you sleep well?" he asked softly.

She looked up from her coffee cup, a bit of her resentment melting as he searched her eyes with a warm, caressing gaze. "Yes," she admitted. "Must be this clean country air."

He smiled. "I slept better than I have in years." His hand moved across the kitchen table to close gently over hers. She trembled at his easy, possessive touch, wanting to pull away, but somehow unable to. "I wish we could stay longer," he said. "But we've got to hit the road within the hour. Think you can manage it?"

"No problem," she said, taking her hand away and awkwardly picking up a fork. On the road, on the road. And when the road came to an end?

"What are you thinking?" he asked, his eyes probing her averted gaze.

"Oh... thinking about traveling," she said, with forced casualness. "It's such second nature to you. I'm used to staying longer in one place."

She met his eyes again as she chewed her eggs. The velvet depths of his gaze seemed to darken as she watched. "I wondered if you'd go off on this tack," he said quietly. "The morning after."

"What tack is that?"

"Focusing on our differences again. Looking for problems, looking for trouble."

"I'm not looking for trouble," she said. It came looking for me, she added mentally.

"There shouldn't be any," he said evenly. "Kelly—love—what's on your mind?"

She stared at him, not knowing what to say. She wanted him to say it—to tell her again that the love was real, that she was so important to him that any plans he'd been making would include her from now on.

"Regrets?" he asked softly.

But that would be asking—expecting—too much, she realized. "No," she sighed. "No regrets."

He cocked his head, as if listening to her unspoken thoughts, his eyes searching hers. "It's been wonderful, being with you," he said, the low husky rasp in his voice bringing a catch to her throat. "It can only get better," he went on. "We've got a lot ahead of us."

Do we? she wondered. How much? She looked away. Oh, why couldn't she be like he was—willing to take a casual fling for what it was, living in the present, enjoying what was there to enjoy, not caring about the consequences? Was she the fool for wanting more?

"I suppose," she said, affecting cheerfulness with some difficulty. "Then I'd better eat this up in a hurry, shower, and get dressed. What time are we due in Denver?"

He looked at her sharply, and that hurt expression she'd seen only once before—or imagined she'd seen—reappeared for an instant, then vanished. "The conference starts at sundown," he said slowly, after a moment. "It's a four- or five-hour drive from here."

She nodded, digging into her eggs. "Okay," she said. "I'll be ready in no time."

"Kelly—"

She looked up again. Julian appeared to be forming a question, and whatever it was indicated some inner struggle. "Yes?"

At the matter-of-fact tone in her voice, and the forcedly cool expression on her face, he reconsidered, and merely shook his head. "You don't have to act this way," he muttered.

"I'm sorry," she said. "I tend to be less affectionate when I haven't had my morning coffee."

He narrowed his eyes at her. "So it seems," he murmured, then rose from the table. "Well, I'm going to ready up the trailer."

Kelly nodded, her mouth full. Only when she was alone again in the kitchen did a deep shuddering breath escape her, and she sat back in the chair, her appetite gone. Did she have to play it this way, to protect herself—pretend that nothing mattered, that her feelings were still unaffected? She sighed, staring down at the table. She didn't even know what game she was playing, exactly.

The screen door opened and slammed. Startled, Kelly looked up to see Annie hovering by the table, a paper bag cradled in her arms.

"Good morning." Annie smiled. "How're you doing?"

"Fine," Kelly lied, trying to put on as convincing a smile as she could manage.

"You sure?" Annie peered at her more closely, with a look of concern.

"I guess I didn't get enough sleep," Kelly said. "That's all."

"That's not necessarily a reason for looking glum," Annie said. Then, seeing Kelly's embarrassed look, she added quickly, "Sorry! Don't mean to get personal. Here, these are for you." She held out the bag. Kelly took it, and looking within saw a dozen large, ripe tomatoes. "Just picked 'em outside," Annie said. "Something for the road."

"Thanks, Annie." Kelly smiled. "Thanks for everything. I . . . I wish I could stay a little longer."

"Yeah, I wish you could, too," Annie replied. "I like what you're doing for Julian."

"Me?" Kelly stared at her. "What do you mean?"

Annie shrugged. "He looks good. He's got a kind of glow—least he did when I saw him before. If you ask me, he's head over heels . . ." She stopped. "But you didn't ask me. Anyway—good luck, you know, with your article and everything. I've got to go into town, so I'll probably miss you on your way out." She reached across the table to give Kelly's hand a friendly pat.

"It's been good to meet you, Annie," Kelly told her.

"Same here." Annie smiled, turned, then paused by the door. "He's a tough one, Kelly. Julian doesn't exactly wear his heart on his sleeve..."

"I think I know what you mean," Kelly said slowly. "I was beginning to wonder... if it was worth the trouble—" She paused, feeling self-conscious.

"Oh, he's worth *some* trouble, I think," Annie said wryly. "And if he's too much trouble in the long run—well, enjoy it while it lasts, I always say. But then, that's me." Chuckling, she shook her head. "Take care, Kelly. Hope we see you again." With a smile and a wave, she was out the door.

Kelly sat staring after her, considering the philosophy of Annie while she sipped her coffee. Could she learn to be so carefree—now, when she was already so in love? The doubt lay heavy on her heart.

As they approached the Colorado border, the countryside she watched fly by was the most hauntingly "western" she'd seen so far: wide open spaces of green and yellow fields sloping to distant mountains; passes through sheer broken hills of rock with rainbow striations glinting in the sun; the sky a deep blue laced with storybook-fluffy white clouds; and the first appearance of sea-green cacti poking their stubborn prickly arms heavenward at the side of the road. She saw a lot of the scenery, and she was able to give it a great deal of her attention, because conversation was scarce.

It felt so strange to regain her seat next to Julian in the trailer. It seemed oddly empty without Siegfried aboard. And so much had changed between the taciturn magician and her, the staunchly uninvolved journalist, in so short a time. Kelly felt as if the rug had been pulled out from underneath her. Just when they'd become so close, they were suddenly so distant.

Kelly stole a glance at Julian, his face implacable beneath his sunglasses. After his initial confusion at her reserved manner, he'd become somewhat stony-faced himself. She wondered if he now regretted those brief hours of vulnerability when he'd whispered his inner thoughts and dreams to her in the midst of a warm embrace. Was she being deliberately cruel by cutting off her own feelings toward him so methodically? But then, had any of it been real, on his side? Hadn't he just been paying lip service to the idea of really forming a commitment?

As she watched, he glanced at her, stroking one end of his mustache in a characteristic gesture of amusement. "So," he said, "if you don't mind my breaking up this lively conversation with some professional matters—do you feel prepared to meet Wolfgang again?"

"Prepared?" She looked out through the windshield, where the sun was starting to sink lower over the distant mountains. "Well, I think so. I've got the camera loaded, and the tape recorder. And you've told me what to look for."

"But you'll be alone this time," he reminded her. "Maybe we should go over some things."

"All right." It was easier to drop back into this mode again—he the purveyor of information, she the studious journalist, boning up on magic tricks as if studying for an exam. For a half hour or so, they examined Wolfgang's psychic feats, as they had before, from every angle, Julian pointing out the most probable methods of subterfuge the conjurer would use to create the illusion of supernatural "powers."

"Okay," he said, as they rode toward a Technicolor vista of sunset that looked like the painted backdrop of a Western movie. "Sounds like we're in good shape."

I wouldn't go that far, she answered mentally. We're not in any shape at all. As if reading her mind, he chuckled to himself, shaking his head.

"Haven't we had enough of this professionalism for a while?" he asked. "Kelly—do you think you could tell me the reason why you're acting like we've barely been introduced, let alone slept together?"

Kelly sighed, her eyes fixed on the glorious scenery. "I

Under His Spell 133

just think it's better that we put last night behind us," she said slowly.

"Why is it better?" came his quiet rejoinder.

"It's just... easier for me to handle," she said finally. "Look, I told you when we started this trip that I wasn't interested in any sort of involvement. That hasn't changed."

"It hasn't?" He shook his head. "I don't understand you."

"We're still the same people," she went on. *"You* haven't changed," she added pointedly.

"I feel I have," he said. "But the way you continue to mistrust me isn't helping things."

Again she was tempted to confront him directly, but she hesitated. If she accused him of betraying her with false promises, he'd most likely try to smooth things over with more of the same. Just a short tour—just another gig—that's what Richard had always said. And then things would settle down... But they never had.

"Maybe I'm not interested in helping things," she said tersely. "Look, things were fine between us before we... before last night. We were becoming... friends. That feels comfortable to me."

"Comfortable?" He sounded incredulous. "You must be made of..." His voice trailed off. He shook his head. "If that's the way you want it." He pursed his lips, then frowned, squinting at the falling sun. "But everything I've said to you, I've meant," he said quietly. "I think you're being self-destructive."

"Spare me the psychological analysis," she retorted. "I'm just looking out for myself. As you are."

"You know me so well." His voice was bitterly ironic.

Kelly bit her lip, unable to say more. The hurt feeling that had stung her so that morning was returning, and she looked away, the countryside blurring in her window. They rode on in silence, the few feet between them now a gulf of many miles.

The camera snuggled in her lap beneath conference brochures felt as if it might burn a hole in her dress. So far, she had been able to snap half a dozen photos without lifting the camera to her eye. The super-small apparatus was fitted with a wide-angle lens, which, with some practice, she was able to point well enough to get, she hoped, the incriminating evidence she needed. Photos and recordings were of course not allowed while Wolfgang demonstrated his powers—as they apparently disturbed his psychic concentration.

Her focus for most of this performance was Fritz Murnau—because it was Julian's supposition that Fritz acted as Wolfgang's confederate.

Now she watched the bearded man closely as he sat in the front row, roughly opposite the psychic on the stage. From her vantage point, she could see his every gesture. Wolfgang was blindfolded, "reading" the numbers an assistant wrote on a blackboard nearby and erased before the blindfold was lowered. If Julian's suspicions were correct, Wolfgang was "told" the number the assistant had written by Fritz's enacting a prearranged code.

"I'm getting an image of an eight," Wolfgang intoned, as people around her murmured in anticipation. She kept her eyes on Fritz, and the camera. "Yes, the number is eighty..." He squinted, as if concentrating. Fritz scratched his nose.

Her camera clicked quietly.

"Eighty-two," said Wolfgang. The audience applauded.

Later, with the tape that was silently unreeling in her handbag, she would compare each number the psychic had correctly "read" with the gestures she'd noted on Fritz's part—seemingly random, insignificant things such as the crossing and uncrossing of his legs, the casual rubbing of a left or right ear. With Julian's help, she hoped to break the code...

With Julian. Once again her mind wandered from the psychic on the stage to the magician somewhere on the streets of Denver. Again, she felt the aching tug within her at the thought of him. She was feeling their brief separation even more keenly than she could have imagined. How had the man managed to insinuate himself into her very bloodstream like this, in such a short amount of time? Why, now that she was no longer with him, did all her resentments and recriminations seem to fade away?

As she pictured him, she could see only his beautiful long fingers gliding over her skin in the darkness. She heard his soft, whispered longings in her ear with a clarity that brought a flush to her face, as she relived the intimacies of the night before again, remembering the scent of him, the feel of him...

Kelly struggled to concentrate on the stage. Amid applause, Wolfgang had removed the blindfold for good, and was standing at the podium, asking for someone in the audience to come forward. Nervous laughs and titters sounded in the seats around her, as friends tried to force their friends to volunteer. Wolfgang was going to bend metal—some object that a volunteer would give him.

Kelly twitched uncomfortably in her seat. Maybe she *was* a fool not to take what Julian was offering her: fun, excitement, the kind of pleasure that had eluded her for so long since her time with Richard—the kind of pleasure, she reflected, with an instinctive shiver, that even Richard had never given her. Could she learn to put her heart under wraps—to let go and just enjoy this devastating man with no strings attached? If only her heart wasn't so full of him already!

She sighed, leaning back in her seat. If she and Julian were going to be spending more time together, as they assuredly would be, this constant pretending not to care, not to be missing his affectionate touch, his soft kisses, was promising to be torturous...

These thoughts stayed with her as the performance continued. Dutifully she fulfilled her task, realizing at every juncture that she was doing it all as much for Julian as for herself. She wanted him to be proud of her work. With every possible clue to Wolfgang's quackery that she gathered, she felt his unseen presence, and anticipated sharing the excitement of their unraveling detective work together.

Afterward, before going backstage to further ingratiate herself with the psychic and his assistant, and consolidate, she hoped, an invitation to the testing sessions in San Diego,

Kelly stopped in a phone booth to check with Bruce Perlstein in New York. She knew that by now her colleague would be knee-deep in foreign periodical clippings, and she hoped he'd been able to unearth some kind of background material on Wolfgang that might fill in one of the gaps in the psychic's murky past.

"Bruce is away from his desk," Penny, his assistant, told her when the call went through. "But I know he wants to talk to you—so can you hold on? How's it going out there, anyway?"

Kelly chatted with Penny as they waited for Bruce's return. She found to her chagrin that the office suddenly seemed light-years away. All of the inner-office goings-on and gossip that Penny garrulously conveyed appeared insignificant to her; Albert's latest temper tantrum bored her, and the entire *Omnibus* world appeared shrunken to pea size.

That's what comes from riding a leopard bare-legged in the moonlight, she mused ruefully, and her heart gave another tug. Annie's words came back to her: enjoy it while it lasts. If only she could—take this special, exhilarating time with Julian for what it was—as a sort of delirious, sensual holiday...

"Kelly!" Bruce's voice from across the country crackled with excitement, and Kelly was jolted back to the present. "I've been waiting for your call. I think we've struck pay dirt here."

The door to the trailer hissed open for her at a residential corner they'd selected earlier for their rendezvous. Kelly took the steps two at a time. Breathlessly, she dropped her bags in the aisle with a clatter and slid into her seat as Julian gazed at her, bemused.

"Sharpe, we're in business," she said, beaming.

"What did you do? Catch him with a pre-bent key red-handed?"

"No, something more interesting than that." She bent over, rummaging in her bag for the camera and tape recorder.

Under His Spell   137

"So, out with it, Kelly—what gives?" he asked impatiently, turning on the engine.

She looked at him, relishing her moment of triumph and his impatience to hear her news. "Well, first of all," she said, "I've got permission for San Diego."

"Fantastic," he said. "I knew you could manage that. And—?"

"And I think you're dead-on about that code Wolfgang's got worked out with Fritz. I've never seen a man rub his ears, cross his legs, and tweak his own nose so much in a ten-minute period. I took photos and I ran the tape..." She'd pulled the equipment out now and brandished it at Julian.

"Excellent." He nodded, easing into the deserted street, whose sole streetlamp illuminated broad palm fronds outside a Spanish ranch-style suburban house.

"But I talked to my office before I went to see Wolfgang—and Bruce has gotten hold of something that's priceless." She paused dramatically.

"Kelly Robbins, if you don't stop beating around the bush, I swear I'll pull over and spank the information out of you."

"Kinky!" She widened her eyes at him. "You'd like that, wouldn't you?"

Julian sighed. "Kelly..."

"Okay. Here's the scoop. Bruce has found a newspaper review, dated eight years back, of a magic show in Stuttgart, featuring an extremely talented sleight-of-hand conjurer who went by the name of Wolfgang Bausch—"

"You're kidding." Julian pulled over to the curb again, brakes squealing. "Are you sure—"

"Everything about the man fits except the last name—bending metal, reading through sealed envelopes, guessing figures, making a watch move—all the basic tricks are there."

"Bruce thinks it's the same man?"

"He's doing more checking. But it looks good...and if we can verify it—"

"Then we've got tangible proof that our supposedly gifted

'natural' is actually a trained magician," Julian said. "Wouldn't that be nice?"

"Yes, it would be," she said, smiling.

"This is the sort of thing I like to hear," he said, pulling back into the street again, nodding his head with a grin. "Damn!" He hit the steering wheel with an emphatic fist, then turned to look at Kelly. "You've done a good job tonight—and your staff's not bad either."

"Thank you," she said. "Oh, don't stop—I'll take as much praise as you're willing to give."

"Well," he went on, "you've done a professional job, so far."

"High praise indeed," she noted.

"I'd also say you're the best long-distance eyes and ears I've ever worked with. The best-looking eyes and ears, as well—"

"So we're back to mere flattery?" she teased. Nonetheless, she was enjoying this flirtatious banter. Their mutual high spirits had dispelled—at least for the moment—the uneasy mistrust of the afternoon.

"I think we should celebrate," he said, absently fingering his mustache.

"Isn't it a little early?"

"Never too early for a celebration—that's what my father used to say." He grinned. "Although that often meant he'd be taking a little nip before the sun was down... But anyway, what would you say to a drink? Some champagne?"

"I'm too well bred to refuse," Kelly answered. "Got any handy?"

"No," he said, brow furrowing in thought. "But I know where we could get that and a whole lot more." He turned sharply, heading across a busier downtown thoroughfare and bearing west, toward the mountains.

"The San Diego testing is still the most important key," Kelly mused aloud. She was savoring the feeling of camaraderie and teamwork that had been brought back by her successful night. With the tension between them broken by her good news and Julian's jubilant reaction, she could almost imagine the two of them getting along as they had before.

"San Diego's the acid test," he agreed. "I have some strategies for that, and a few tricks up my own sleeve..." He shot Kelly a mischievous smile. "But we can discuss that later in the evening. Now we should just concentrate on feeling good—don't you think?"

"I'd like to," she sighed. "Julian..."

"Look," he said, "I know it's been a tense day. I guess I've been reacting to those 'Private—Keep Out' signs you've been wearing since this morning—"

"I'm sorry," she said. "It's just not easy for me...to..." The idea of dredging up the issue of his tour in the fall and whether there was really a future for them together seemed suddenly too weighty to broach. Just when they were feeling comfortable together for the first time all day, she didn't want to provoke another argument.

"To open up?" he suggested, finishing her sentence for her as she let it hang. "I think I know a little bit about how difficult that can be."

Kelly looked at him, measuring the sincerity of his words. When he said something as direct and revealing as that, it was difficult to see any deceit in him. Instead, she could only see the softness of his eyes, remember the warmth of his touch. Was she too far gone already to have any perspective? It was so tempting to believe he really cared about her, felt about her the way she was feeling for him.

"I'm a little rusty on being vulnerable," she admitted. "I think last night...made me feel that way. And this morning—"

"You wished you hadn't?" He glanced at her, then nodded as if to himself. "But I'm glad you let yourself go, with me. What we shared together last night was a very special thing."

"I thought so," she said carefully. The doubts and questions hovered on the tip of her tongue once more. Oh, Kelly, she groaned inwardly—why can't you just leave well enough alone? Why do we have to have everything tied up in a little bow—love with security, guarantees written in stone?

"It meant a lot to me," he said softly, then cleared his throat, as if embarrassed by the confession. "But I'm willing to go easy—to take things one step at a time, if that's the way you want it."

"You mean one night at a time?" she couldn't stop herself from asking.

His eyes narrowed as he watched the road. They seemed farther from civilization now, winding slowly around the edges of the mountains. "Does it bother you so much that I'm attracted to you? Why is it wrong for me to want to love you again the way I did last night?" He didn't sound angry, only genuinely perplexed. "God, Kelly, when I think of how good it felt to be with you at last, to hold you in my arms..."

His words were sending a ticklish tendril of arousal through her, conjuring up the images she'd been seeing, feeling, remembering all day, even as she struggled to close herself off from him. "I know," she said softly.

"Then why try to pretend that you don't want it, too?"

Kelly exhaled sharply, closing her eyes against the tumult of erotic imagery. She felt the bus slowing, and the rattle of gravel underneath them brought her upright in her seat. Julian was unbuckling his seat belt, and, leaving the motor running, he knelt quickly at her side.

"Kelly," he said, his eyes glowing with desire, his face only inches from hers, "come back..."

His lips covered hers swiftly. Even as she started to pull away from him it was too late. Her own lips pressed hungrily to his, an answering jolt of desire coursing through her, the hands she lifted to push him away settling about his neck.

It was like an addiction, she thought hazily, as their lips parted at last. She could resist and rationalize, mistrust him and deny her own feelings, but when Julian kissed her, what she felt right then was all that could possibly matter.

"You're—very convincing," she murmured huskily.

His eyes were dark with desire. "Let's spend the night together," he whispered. "Let's make love again...and again..."

Under His Spell 141

His hands on her shoulders seemed to burn through the material of her shirt, and an answering quiver of heat arose within her at his words. Wordlessly, she shook her head in a halfhearted denial.

"Say yes," he whispered. "I've got to have you—now—"

"Here?" she gasped, incredulous.

A brief glance out the window showed her they were pulled over to the side of the road in the midst of nowhere, a sole cactus tree in the trailer's headlights the only visible scenery.

"No." Julian smiled. "But I know a place. We're nearly there."

"What do you mean?" she asked, confused.

"The Rocky Ledge Inn," he said. "This time of year I think we could get in at short notice—"

"Julian Sharpe," she began indignantly. "Do you mean you were already taking me to a hotel, without—"

"For champagne, yes!" he protested. "It was the nicest place I knew of. But why not spend the night? Look, we could get separate rooms, if you insist..."

Torn, she stared into his inviting eyes. With an inward shiver, she realized she was too far gone to deny herself another night of love. One night, she reflected. And whether it was the only night, or one of many—why shouldn't it be hers? Why couldn't she, for once, surrender to the reckless impulse of the moment—and savor that moment, as long as it might last?

"No," she said quietly.

His eyes widened. "No?"

She shook her head with a smile of resignation. "I mean, no, Julian—we don't have to get separate rooms..."

The inn was too far from Colorado's major slopes to qualify as a ski resort, but true to its name, it jutted out on a mountain promontory that offered a breathtaking view of the valleys below. Kelly turned from the rounded picture window after drinking in the moonlit vista in the room's semidarkness. Julian had purposefully left the lights off when they entered so that she could see the land below the ledge.

"It's incredible," she agreed. "When did you stay here before?"

"A few years back," he told her, then spoke into the phone. "Is the bar still open?" As he talked to the person at the front desk, Kelly walked around the room, admiring the Spanish ranch-style motifs—broad wooden beams across the ceiling of dark wood, colorful tile on the floor and soft rugs, the bed set back into a wall of slate stone that faced the panoramic view.

She sat on the bed to test its softness. As it sank beneath her she lay back with a contented sigh. The bed creaked quietly as Julian joined her, stretching out beside her, his arm sliding around her to pull her closer in the dark.

"How do you like it?"

"I like it fine," she said, looking up at him with a tremor of anticipation. As if telepathically receiving her unspoken wish, he bent quickly to kiss her, on the lips, cheeks, and eyelids, until her entire face seemed to tingle from the warm, moist caress of his lips.

"You're sure you don't want your own room, then?" he teased, his hand gently caressing the curve of her hip beneath her jeans.

"Ask me again in a little while," she teased back. "It depends on how strong a spell you weave..."

There was a soft knock on the door to their room. "Well, I'll admit to calling upon some assistance for the spell-casting," he said, rising.

"You have a Fritz of your own?"

He chuckled, heading for the door. "No, something more Continental than Germanic..."

He'd ordered Dom Pérignon, some cheese, and fruit. The taste of the crisp, bubbly champagne was exquisite on her thirsty tongue. Alone in the spacious, rustically elegant room, they drank toast after toast in quick succession, alternating sips with lingering kisses, as they stretched out on a soft rug by the window.

"I think," she said dreamily, after swallowing the fresh

Under His Spell   143

strawberry he'd dangled before her lips, "you've succeeded in keeping me immobile."

"That's the idea," he murmured. "You deserve some pampering after your superior detective work."

"It's nice to be pampered," she mused. Her resolution to live in the present for a night seemed to be paying off quite handsomely. "I could get used to this kind of living," she went on. "A little decadent, but so inviting..."

"Is there anything else you need?" he asked, then arched a mischievous eyebrow. "Or want...?"

"Actually, I could use a nice hot shower," she said.

"I'll go you one better." Julian sat up and took her hand. "Come this way." As he lifted her from the floor, Kelly could feel the effects of the champagne more intensely. She seemed to float, rather than walk, as she let Julian guide her to the bathroom.

"Sauna," he announced, indicating the little room of unvarnished wood built into the spacious bath space. "Then shower."

"Well, it seems a properly healthy, Colorado thing to do," she agreed. Julian switched on a control by the little wooden door, then reached in to pick up the pail within. Filling it with water, he replaced it, checking the setting on the sauna.

"It takes a few minutes to get up to the proper temperature," he said. "I'll bring in the champagne."

When he returned, Kelly had slipped out of her clothes, and was tying a white hotel towel around her. As she pinned her hair up, she caught sight of Julian behind her, stripping off his shirt. She was unable to take her eyes away from his reflection as he unzipped and then removed his pants. The casual intimacy of his undressing brought a knot of heated arousal to her stomach.

Then, towel around his waist, Julian was ushering her into the sauna, champagne and glasses in both hands. The little room was just big enough for the two of them to stretch out opposite each other on the wooden platforms. Julian poured them each a fresh glass.

The cool champagne was a delicious contrast to the hot,

steamy air of the little room. The steam rose in intensity as Julian splashed water on the heated rocks in a bin on the wall beside him. Kelly closed her eyes, luxuriating in the feel of her skin's pores opening and cleansing in the moist heat.

After a few minutes, sweat was trickling down between her breasts and thighs. As she heard the clink of Julian's replenishing her glass, she stole a glance at his tanned and beautifully toned physique in repose. The sweat sliding down his broad and curly-haired chest caught her eye. She followed a rivulet as it slowly descended to the towel loosely slung about his hips, then closed her eyes again as heat seemed to suffuse her from both outside and within.

In a few more minutes, she could stand it no more. Julian rose as she did, wordlessly nodding. They stepped out onto the bathroom's Spanish tile. Julian turned the shower on full blast and turned to face her, sweat trickling down his high cheekbones, beaded on his mustache.

"Come with me," he said simply. He undid the corner of his towel and reached in an easy movement to untie hers. They stood facing each other, eyes locking, and Kelly realized she had never felt as bold in her nakedness, as unashamed, as when he looked at her, with open admiration and desire in his eyes.

Then he was helping her into the white-tiled shower stall, its base a low porcelain tub, with plenty of room for them to stand together under the gushing jets of wonderfully cool water. The door slid closed behind them, and they faced each other in the rushing torrent. With a grin, Julian pulled her directly beneath the spout, laughing as she sputtered under the deluge.

With soap in hand, he began to wash her, slowly massaging her with the sweetly scented bar and his nimble fingers, covering her skin with suds. The sensual feel of the slippery soap and his naked skin against hers as he stepped closer were arousing her to breathless anticipation, but he moved with slow, languid strokes, carefully massaging her neck and shoulders, taking his time as her muscles quivered and then relaxed beneath his skillful fingers.

Under His Spell

Soon she was a trembling mass of tingling limbs beside him, wholly in his power, her breath coming slowly and deeply as he turned her around in the warm, wet torrent, his hands slipping now to caress and explore more intimate places. A moan of pleasure escaped her trembling lips as his hands lifted and kneaded her breasts, soapy fingers teasing the rosy points to aching erection.

The evidence of his own arousal was hard and warm against the slope of her buttocks as she leaned back against him. Julian kissed and licked her neck as his hands traveled slowly over the curve of her belly, to play with the wet tangle of hair at the juncture of her thighs. She thought she might go crazy with anticipation as he probed and teased the swelling moist tenderness below.

Then she turned suddenly, filled with the desire to regain control, to bring him panting to the brink of unbearable pleasure as he had seduced her. Grabbing the soap from the tub side, she began to spread suds over his fuzzy mass of chest hair. Smiling, he relaxed beneath her slippery hands, which spread in widening circles on his chest, then began a tantalizing descent.

It was equally arousing to feel him tense and relax under her skilled manipulation. She lingered lovingly over the powerful muscles of his hips, the small of his back, pulling him into the water's flow as she massaged his supple shoulders and neck. Then, facing him again, she soaped and caressed his legs, thighs, and the sensitive valley between hip and thigh, until it was he who moaned, shivering at her exploring caresses. Sensual skills that his own abandon had awakened in her rose instinctively as she stroked and fondled him, her own desire growing as she aroused his.

At last, with a strangled groan he pulled her to him, covering her wet lips with his, drawing her full slippery length against his in the warm torrent. Their skin seemed to melt as their tongues met in the waterfall-like downpour, and she reeled with mounting, heady pleasure as their kiss deepened, growing more urgent.

Then, leaning back against the tile, his darkly tanned skin a sensuous contrast to the bright white surface, Julian grasped her by the hips, gently guiding her into position as the water splashed down between them. Trembling with the exquisite pleasure of their slippery, tantalizingly slow movements toward union, she sank down to receive him, the water covering her shoulders and neck in a warm and wet cascade.

"Careful," he murmured huskily, as she began to move against him, her breath coming faster, in shuddering gasps.

"Yes," she breathed. "Oh... this is... dangerous, isn't it?"

Slowly, he shook his head from side to side, chin jutting upward as their legs interlocked. "You're... in good hands," he breathed.

"I believe you," she murmured.

He smiled. "Watching you... is wonderful..." he whispered. "My little water nymph..."

She arched her back, loving the feel of the water and his hands cupping her buttocks as they rose and fell slowly in his grasp. "I always... seem... to end up wet... when I'm with you," she murmured.

"I've noticed..." he said, looking at her from between sultry, half-closed eyelids. "Are you... naturally aquatic?"

"To tell you the truth..."—she made an instinctive sighing sound of satisfaction as he pulled her even closer, her body trembling from the impact of his slow, exquisite thrusts—"... I've never done this before, either."

His eyes opened wider. "No? Then you really are... a natural."

"And you?"

"I'm just a man in love," he whispered, his eyes glimmering as he held her gaze. "You bring out the adventurer in me..."

Then all conversation ceased. As their lips came together once more in the splashing torrents, she felt her last lingering fears dissolving in a wave of mounting, exultant joy.

Chapter 8

LATER, LOUNGING ON the bed, sharing an apple with Julian as soft symphonic music played on the radio nearby, Kelly felt as if she had been split in two. One of her was the devil-may-care, naked, and abandoned woman who lay by her lover's side, smiling as he lazily fed her another slice of apple; the other was watching the whole scene as if from the wrong end of a telescope, worried and reproachful, removed, judgmental—a disembodied conscience that whispered in her ear: Faker. You think it's fine to go on like this. You think you're strong enough to sail through your little fling and land on your feet? Sure! Pretend you don't care. Pretend one night is enough, that it isn't love you're feeling for him... and when it's over? Think you'll be able to pretend that having loved again and lost won't hurt? Fool, fool, fool...

Kelly closed her eyes, sighing. If only she could quiet that voice in her head. If only she could readjust this odd double vision she was having—relax, and live only in the present moment...

Julian's gentle caress on her hip made her open her eyes once more. He was holding up the half of the apple they hadn't yet eaten.

"Isn't this supposed to come first, historically?" he asked.

Kelly smiled. Julian Sharpe certainly didn't have any trouble adjusting to this kind of life-style. "Yes, we have done it backward, haven't we?" she mused, happy to slip back into idle, flippant banter.

"No, actually, we haven't yet," he said, with a lascivious grin, and she took a mock swing at him.

"So," she said, munching on the apple, "I guess we've

proved conclusively that you're incapable of maintaining mere friendship with a woman you're attracted to."

"We've proved more than that."

"Such as?"

"Well," he began, cutting another slice, "we've proved that you're incapable of maintaining a purely professional relationship with a man you're attracted to."

"Unfair," she said. "This is a special case."

"For me, too," he said quietly. The soft seriousness in his tone as he brought his hand to gently caress hers touched her to the core. Could she have been wrong? she wondered. Maybe she'd judged him too quickly. Maybe there was more to his intentions, after all... And she was trying so hard to perceive their relationship as a casual fling, to play the part of the carefree bedmate. Wouldn't it be wonderful if...

"Well, I'm certainly not used to nudist journalism," she joked. "If Albert could see me now..."

"He'd most likely drop his pipe," suggested Julian.

"Wait till he sees my traveling expenses." She grimaced. "Which reminds me—I forgot to bring in my overnight bag." She looked around. "No, don't get up—I'll get it," she told him, as he began to rise. "I could use a little cool night air to clear this erotic haze from my head."

"Poetry," he said, shaking his head. "I'm telling you, you ought to—"

"Please," she sighed. "Now, what happened to my clothes? You know, I remember a time when I used to keep them on for more than a few minutes at a stretch..."

It did feel good to walk out under the stars again in the fresh air. Clambering into the trailer she felt wonderfully woozy, tired but still energetic. The trailer that had seemed such an odd domicile just a week ago seemed warm and homey to her now as she walked down the aisle. But her bag wasn't where she remembered Julian stowing it. So she turned on the lights in the back compartment.

There it was, by the desk. As she hoisted the bag over one shoulder and reached across the desk to turn the lamp off, her attention was arrested by a black folder she hadn't noticed before, lying there with a matte knife and glue stick atop it.

A scrapbook, no doubt. Curious, Kelly put the bag down and opened the folder, idly turning the glossy black pages.

Within a few minutes, she sat down slowly, all wooziness gone. With each turn of a page, her heart hammered a little more forcefully—each glossy photograph in succession like little nails in the coffin of her dreams.

Because on nearly every page, in a picture-perfect parade, various and sundry females could be seen with Julian and James. There was a blonde on Julian's arm... a brunette in his lap... two auburn-haired twins, even, to round out the assortment, sitting with easy familiarity on either side of the handsome magician beneath a banner proclaiming their show's arrival in Cincinnati.

Kelly closed the book with an abrupt bang, her mind whirling.

Lord, it was like a collection—a veritable trophy wall in bound form. She'd lost count after ten, the various faces and bodies—all quite alluring, she couldn't help noting—melding together in her eyes as she'd turned the pages. And these sensuous tour souvenirs seemed to span from coast to coast as they did year to year...

The thought of this line of feminine companionship stretching into infinity, like the road stretching to the horizon, sickened her.

And she was a special case?

What, she wondered, her stomach lurching queasily as her emotions seethed, was there about her that could possibly be so special? That she'd taken a little longer to come around?

As she walked slowly up the darkened aisle of the bus, her bag swinging limply at her side, she tried briefly to rationalize the contents of the Pandora's box she'd just opened, but nothing convincing came to mind. Her first instincts had been correct. Julian was another Richard, or worse—Richard had at least admitted he was an unabashed philanderer.

The conversation she'd overheard in the kitchen came back to her again with renewed clarity. She'd been trying to forget it, repress it, twist its meaning to fit her own fantasy, but now she couldn't pretend. Of course he was going off on another tour. Spending a brief week with her hadn't changed a thing about the man. Who was she trying to kid?

Only herself. She felt sickened now at her own self-deception. Sure, she'd tried to pretend it was all right to play it "casual," that she could handle a seemingly futureless affair with Julian. But in truth, a part of her had been hoping, fervently, that there was more to it; a trusting part of her had still believed his words of love, secretly wishing he wanted her as she wanted him... Now their idyll of tender passion looked like just another tawdry one-night stop on his endless road.

When she unlocked the door to their room, Julian was sprawled comfortably across the bed, her tape recorder beside him and the headphones on. Eyes closed, he smiled faintly as she came in, obviously amused at the recording of Wolfgang's performance. When Kelly dropped her bag by the bed with a dull thud, he opened his eyes and sat up.

"He usually fails the first time he tries something," he noted, taking the headphones off. "That way he seems more like the real thing. But he bent the old lady's bracelet?" he asked her. "On the second try?"

Kelly nodded. With cynical eyes now she appraised Julian's physique. A man as well built as he was could only be catnip to the ladies. His self-assurance in his physical presence was well founded. Suppressing a sigh, Kelly tore her eyes from his handsome nudity, her stomach tightening into a little ball of jealousy and remorse.

"Well, I think it's time to activate my Plan A," he said, switching off the tape. "I've got something special in mind for San Diego that we should go over before we hit the hay..." His voice trailed off as he registered Kelly's tense expression. "What's wrong?"

"Not much," she said, sitting listlessly on the chair across from the bed. "Go on. I'm interested in all of your plans—

especially the ones that go into effect *after* San Diego."

"After?" He looked at her, puzzled. "What do you mean?"

"I mean when the show's over," she said tersely. "What then?"

Julian's eyes narrowed. He swung his legs over the side of the bed and picked up the towel lying there, draping it across his lap. "I have this odd impression," he began slowly, "that one Kelly Robbins walked out of here a few minutes ago, and another one just came in. Did something happen to you in the parking lot?"

"Do you have plans to return with me to New York?" she asked abruptly, ignoring his question.

"If it's necessary," he said, the guardedness she hadn't seen in his manner for some time returning under her accusing stare.

"For the article, you mean?"

"That's right."

"And us?"

"I figured that was something you and I would discuss," he said quietly.

"You mean, right around the time when you showed me the door?"

Julian knotted the towel around his waist, a grim expression on his face. "Kelly, what are you doing? We've been having such a wonderful night together, and now—"

"So I shouldn't spoil it," she snapped, "with any questions, or any stray thoughts in my pretty little head, other than living it up. Tomorrow be damned—that's the idea, isn't it?"

Julian rose, his face darkening. "This is crazy," he muttered. "I've never known a woman so hellbent on turning a good thing bad before it has a fighting chance. This mistrust of yours—"

"I'm surprised," she interrupted, her anger mounting. "I mean, considering the great variety of women you've known. Or is it that they're usually satisfied with the brief good time they get?"

"What is that supposed to mean?" he challenged, standing over her with his hands on his hips.

"The least you could do is keep your scrapbook under wraps," she blurted out. "I mean, it's a little tacky to leave it lying around for any of your many guests to peruse!"

He stared at her, momentarily bewildered. Then he frowned, his eyes glimmering with restrained anger. "I see," he said. "You've been doing some extracurricular research."

"I'm sorry. I'd been enjoying getting to know you so much, I wanted to know more. Now I wish I'd been less curious," she said bitterly.

"So you formed conclusions awfully fast," he said gruffly. "Isn't it bad form for a journalist to be so rapidly judgmental?"

"What am I supposed to think?" she asked. "Those women are all cousins? Friends of the family? Or—what do you call them—groupies? So that makes it inconsequential?"

"Even if they are whatever you're so willing to think they are, Kelly, why are you so eager to condemn me?" he retorted, his voice rising.

"I'm not condemning you," she said hotly. "You're entitled to the wonderful dividends of the traveling entertainer's life. I just don't like being added to a collection!"

Julian glared at her, his mustache twitching as he struggled to compose his features. With a muttered oath, he slammed the table next to her with his fist, then turned away. Kelly trembled in her seat as if her body had received the blow. Steeled by anger, she nonetheless met his gaze evenly when he turned to face her again.

"You should think more of yourself than that," he said more quietly, a plaintive note in his voice. "You should know that I do."

"I do think more of myself," she said, "which is why I didn't want to get involved with you in the first place. You're a fascinating, attractive man," she went on, when he took a step back as if slapped. "But you're obviously not the kind of man who's interested in a serious relationship."

"You've got me all figured out, I see," he said coolly. "And I guess whatever I've said to you, whatever we've had together, hasn't changed your picture of me."

"What am I supposed to believe?" she cried, rising from her chair. "You say one thing and then you do another—" She stopped, realizing she was going too far to turn back now.

"What have I said that I haven't done?" He stared at her, his eyes smoldering with defiance. "I never claimed I'd been celibate, if that's what you mean."

"All this talk about changing your way of life—how you're thinking about going off the road—writing your book—and then you turn around and start planning the itinerary for your next European tour!"

Julian's eyes widened. Then his features settled into a hardened mask as he faced her, arms folded. "You really are the inquisitive reporter, aren't you? What else have you uncovered about me in our brief trip? Got anything on tape?"

"I couldn't help hearing what you and James were talking about," she said, the stony contempt emanating from his eyes making her inwardly cringe. "I didn't set out to eavesdrop. And I thought—I hoped—"

"You hoped what?" he asked coldly.

"I hoped you'd tell me different!" she exclaimed, her voice breaking. "I wanted you to tell me yourself, to . . . to explain yourself. And then, when I was with you again, I tried to convince myself that it didn't matter, that I didn't care—but . . ."

"So you were testing me," he said, his voice devoid of emotion. "And apparently I failed. Nice to know I've been tried and convicted, and in such record time."

She turned away, overcome by an avalanche of remorse and bitter anger. Julian stalked to the other end of the room. She could hear him putting on his trousers, zipping them up, and buckling them. She covered her face with her hands, fighting back tears. In a few moments, she heard the door shut softly behind him. He was gone.

She could hear his angry steps stalking down the gravel path. Kelly watched the door until the tears dissolved it before her, and she curled up miserably in the chair, her body wracked with anguished sobs.

* * *

After a fitful night of little sleep, Kelly awoke, feeling woefully hung over and not at all happy to be alone. The empty champagne bottle and the rinds of cheese and fruit were painful reminders of the happiness she'd shared with Julian before she'd had the misfortune to walk out to his trailer.

Kelly sighed. Even taking a shower proved to be a discomfiting experience. Images of their erotic idyll kept creeping into her awakening consciousness as she felt the water pounding her shoulders.

She dressed slowly, eyes drifting toward the door. She dawdled, packing up her few belongings, both hesitant to see Julian and yet half wishing he would come in to see her first. After a while, hunger won out over pride. She'd have to face him soon enough, she decided, and having breakfast was as good a reason as any.

When she opened the door of the room, the bright sunlight blinded her momentarily. After her eyes had adjusted to the morning light, she looked to where the trailer had been parked the night before.

Gone.

For a moment she stared in disbelief at the empty parking spot. Then, her heart beating faster, she took a tentative tour of the whole parking area. There was no sign of the Airstream trailer's familiar silver sparkle. More than hunger turning in her stomach, she made her way to the office of the inn. She'd heard what she suspected was Julian pulling out of the lot last night, but she'd thought he'd returned as she drifted into sleep...

The clerk was a long-haired young man in a Hawaiian shirt whose face was ruddy with a ski-slope tan. He nodded amiably as Kelly asked about Mr. Sharpe's whereabouts. "Your friend checked out," he told her, in a lazy, nasal drawl. "Hey, but don't worry, the room's been paid for."

Kelly stared at him, then colored as the man returned her stare with a rather moony grin. "Did he..." Hazily, she tried to order her thoughts, fending off a combination

Under His Spell

of panic and outrage. "Did he leave anything? Any word, or..."

The clerk's grin broadened, and he nodded many times, peering under the counter. "For sure he did," he said, searching methodically through some papers as she stood by, quivering with impatience. "Lemme see, it was like, an envelope..."

At last he produced an envelope that bore her room number in Julian's distinctive scrawl. Ignoring the interested clerk's watchful eyes, she ripped it open. Enclosed were two things: a very brief note, and an airline ticket.

The ticket was a prepaid flight from Denver to San Diego. The note was all of three sentences:

> Sorry we didn't get to discuss those plans—mine or ours. I think it's best for us to go on separately at this point. I'll contact you in California.

It was signed with his initials. Kelly watched the cursive letters blur before her eyes. She closed them. So the magician had pulled a real disappearing act...

Kelly exhaled a deep breath. She turned to face the opened door of the little office, walked to it, and stood staring at the mountains—so beautiful and so indifferent.

Well, she'd always prided herself on being a professional, she thought dully, watching a distant hawk swoop amid the powder blue above craggy peaks. She'd been in straits much more dire than this before, hadn't she? Now all that was in front of her was a job she'd started that she had to finish. When she looked at it that way, it was really simple.

Wasn't it?

Before the aching hurt could overwhelm her, she resolutely threw herself into motion. Business first. She made a series of phone calls, and in another hour she was in a cab en route to the airport, with all the details of the afternoon and night ahead mapped out efficiently. There would be a rented car ready for her at the airport in San Diego, and a reservation booked at The Cabrillo—the big hotel in town that had the additional advantage of putting her under the same roof with Wolfgang Lang and Fritz Murnau, whose itinerary indicated they'd be staying there.

Only when her plane was taxiing down the runway at dusk did she relax the iron grip she'd held on her emotions all day. Her face pale and wan in the little plastic window's reflection as she stared out at the blinking lights, Kelly allowed herself the questionable indulgence of thinking over what had happened to her.

The ticket Julian had left her had been purchased in New York. What did that mean? Had he intended to leave her high and dry from the very start? It didn't seem possible. In vain, she tried to reconstruct the references Julian had made to "a plan" the night before. But she couldn't piece together much more than a sense that it was likely he'd intended for them to reach San Diego separately... or was it? And why?

With a churning rumble, the silver bird took flight. With the throbbing ache inside of her returning full force, Kelly sat back in her seat, her mind whirling relentlessly ahead. The note mentioned "contact." Would he meet her there? Or was he already back in Nebraska? Maybe her accusations had angered him so, or his own guilt was so strong, that he wouldn't contact her at all. Glancing at the empty seat next to her, she was filled with a sudden rage—only to feel the tears well up a moment later as she realized she missed Julian's presence so much it was scary...

Hold on to yourself, she commanded mentally—it's all you have. Push back the pain. Her journalist's mind clicked absurdly through imaginary pages of titles to encapsulate her story: Seduced and Abandoned. Or was *betrayed* a better word? But this childhood game of fighting feelings with metaphors couldn't keep the dam from bursting. She wept.

After napkins from a kindly stewardess and a much-needed drink stemmed the steady flow of tears sometime later, Kelly attempted, once again, to be rational about what had happened. She'd gone in with her eyes open, hadn't she? Well, that's what she got for mixing her personal and professional life, right? Fate, with a knife twist of perverse irony, had delivered her into the arms of a veritable Richard the Second, another Mister Wrong.

She should have run for cover when she saw the mustache.

Numb, her actions methodical, remote-controlled, she arrived, drove, checked in, showered, dressed. And soon enough, Kelly found herself having drinks at the hotel bar with Fritz Murnau, a Dr. Elgar from the Halliford Institute, a reporter from the *Los Angeles Times,* and—making a dramatic entrance after the lights in the bar had mysteriously flickered—Wolfgang Lang himself.

"Miracle," the psychic beamed. "Where I go—these things always happened."

"Happen," Fritz corrected him with a smile, and then he went on to tell all present about the last hotel Wolfgang had stayed in, which had suffered a major power breakdown within an hour of his arrival. It was unintentional, Fritz assured them, but sometimes Wolfgang's aura was so strong that such amazing electromagnetic reactions occurred in his vicinity...

Listening to the continual bombast of Wolfgang's assistant as they sat down together for some more drinks in the hotel's open courtyard café, Kelly was reminded of Julian's ridiculing the scientific mind. Dr. Elgar, who was high up in the institute's hierarchy, fluent in quantum physics and the inventor of complex laser techniques, was nonetheless an awed and seemingly unskeptical audience. Parapsychology and psychic phenomena were apparently his favorite fields of interest. It was he who had invited the psychic for this brief battery of tests under laboratory conditions. But, Kelly noted, even as she expressed the same awed astonishment as the *Times* reporter at each story the Germans told them, the doctor was far from unprejudiced. He obviously *wanted* to believe it, and it was this very quality Julian had talked about in the early leg of their trip: even the most educated of men were susceptible to a first-rate flim-flammer.

Julian. His presence hovered like an invisible spirit, looking over her shoulder, whispering in her ear. It was the Julian in her that stood back from the relaxed social gathering, shrewdly assessing Fritz's determined politicking with the other reporter, then nudging Kelly forward to get further into Lang's good graces. She couldn't stop her magician-mentor's words from echoing in her mind as she drew information out of the scientist and the psychic, piecing together an already suspect scenario: although these institute tests were to be carried out in "laboratory-controlled conditions," the overly friendly Dr. Elgar had already given Fritz Murnau a personal tour of the premises that day. Kelly was surprised at this lapse in judgment by Dr. Elgar. What was to keep the ever-helpful Fritz from using his prior knowledge of the testing environment to help Wolfgang Lang fake his way through the tests?

Keeping all of these thoughts to herself, using her feminine wiles and cashing in on Wolfgang's more-than-friendly interest in her, Kelly succeeded in getting a firm invitation to attend the testing sessions for an hour or so the following afternoon. Her mission accomplished, she retired, a little tipsy and satisfied that things were going well.

Tossing and turning in the starchy-fresh hotel bed, Kelly soon found the effect of the alcohol diminishing, and a dismal blue funk began to descend on her in its wake. She kept missing Julian's warm and arousing body at her side, and then hating herself for missing him. By midnight she was still wide awake, staring out at the palm trees lining the hotel's courtyard. One more day, she told herself. By this time tomorrow night you'll be landing at LaGuardia, and you can put the whole damn assignment under wraps.

If only the feelings in her heart could be so easily laid to rest . . .

"The room is constructed of double-walled steel," Dr. Elgar explained. "Mr. Lang is isolated visually—although we are monitoring him on the VCR system, of course," he went on, gesturing at the small television monitor mounted

Under His Spell

on a table. "And he's sound-shielded. Again, we can hear him, but he cannot hear us."

Kelly nodded, her pen poised over her pad, her eyes sweeping the small lab room. Fritz Murnau stood facing her, leaning casually against the wall that separated them from Wolfgang, whose face, furrowed in concentration, was visible in stark black and white on the television screen. Two other assistants sat on a slightly raised platform, a number of sealed envelopes in a pile before them.

"The drawings were made earlier this morning by other scientists who have no knowledge of the testing procedures," Dr. Elgar continued. "Each envelope contains one such drawing, selected from an unmarked pile of envelopes by me, personally, prior to the beginning of this test. In this manner, with the precautions we've taken, any sensory leakage or unintentional deception has been prevented."

On the monitor, Wolfgang passed his hand over his forehead, frowning with effort. Kelly chewed on her lower lip, watching. Then the door behind her opened, and she was momentarily distracted by the entrance of two men in white smock coats. Dr. Elgar rose immediately to greet the shorter of the men, treating him with the deference one would give a superior.

"Dr. Elgar, this is Dr. Dulles," the shorter man said. "He's interested in observing for a few minutes, and perhaps participating."

Dr. Elgar was obviously surprised, but he didn't protest, shaking the other man's hand nervously. Kelly gave the newcomer a cursory glance. He was bearded and balding, with thick horn-rimmed glasses; otherwise, there was nothing noteworthy about him. Kelly returned her gaze to the monitor.

Wolfgang was now lifting his pen. Slowly, he began to draw on the small pad placed on the desk before him in his little chamber.

Kelly glanced at the raised platform. Both assistants, eyes riveted to the paper in front of them, were apparently "sending" the image they'd pulled from the sealed envelope to the man beyond the double doors.

Silently, Dr. Elgar passed the drawing around. Kelly moved up to look. The men were nodding silently as one of them handed the little, unfolded paper to Kelly. It was a rudimentary, childlike drawing of a sailboat. Kelly looked to the monitor, surreptitiously stealing a glance at Fritz. Fritz, she noticed, had shifted his position only once since she'd entered the room. When the envelope was first opened, he got a look at its contents, then settled back unobtrusively against the wall, arms folded, seemingly uninvolved in the proceedings.

Silently, Wolfgang Lang studied the pad in front of him. Then, with a last stroke of his pen, he settled back in his chair, apparently satisfied. He looked up at the video camera in his room and spoke softly in German.

"He's ready," Fritz acknowledged.

The other men stood back as Dr. Elgar went to the door and unbolted it, then unbolted the second door. Wolfgang Lang entered the testing room, his pad clutched in his hand. Kelly noticed that he was sweating profusely, as he grinned with enthusiastic bravado at her and the doctor. Eagerly, he thrust his drawing into the hands of one assistant, who took it, holding it against the other drawing for comparison.

There was no denying the striking similarity. Wolfgang had drawn a sailboat, unmistakably—its sails were proportionately bigger than those in the test drawing, but the basic shape was the same. A murmur of surprise and appreciation swept through the little room. Kelly kept her eyes on Fritz. He, too, was elated, but she could see nothing in his actions that suggested he was signaling new information to Wolfgang—and, after all, the next envelope had yet to be opened.

"The subject has reproduced the target drawing with remarkable clarity," Dr. Elgar intoned into the tape recorder on the desk. "Envelope number three can be considered a 'hit.'"

Wolfgang was doing everything but beating his chest in glee at his psychic feat. The two assistants were huddled in a whispered conference. One said a few words to Dr. Elgar,

Under His Spell

who nodded, clearing his throat. "Wolfgang," he said, taking the psychic over to the door, "we'd like to do a series, if possible—with you remaining in the other room. We'll target-test three envelopes in succession, and perhaps you could just hold your drawings up for the monitor to see?"

Wolfgang looked to Fritz, who translated more thoroughly. Wolfgang shrugged, apparently unfazed, and after briefly exchanging a few more words in his native tongue with Fritz, he reentered his chamber.

Dr. Elgar folded his arms and looked significantly at the assembled group. Kelly chewed her lower lip, watching Fritz. Suddenly the man whom she'd sized up as Dr. Elgar's boss spoke, and Kelly looked at him curiously.

"Mr. Murnau, I'd like a word with you, if I could," he said with a friendly nod toward Fritz. His name tag identified him as "Professor Landau," Kelly saw now.

Fritz, surprised, looked from one scientist to the next. He opened his mouth to say something, then thought better of it. Kelly put her pad down, her pulse picking up. Clearly, Wolfgang's assistant did not want to leave the room while the testing was in progress. But to protest would arouse suspicion. He was caught, she realized, with a flush of excitement, in a rather untenable position.

Shrugging, Fritz left the room with Professor Landau. Dr. Dulles, his bearded associate, who had remained silent until now, smiled and moved to the very position Fritz had held—standing with his back to the wall between the observers and Wolfgang. He nodded courteously to Dr. Elgar, who, retaining his composure, bid the assistants to proceed.

The next envelope contained a drawing of an apple. Dr. Dulles gave it a cursory glance and resumed his position. On the monitor, Wolfgang made a great show of concentration. After a few minutes, his drawing was complete, and he held it up for the camera to transmit.

He had drawn a cat. It was a decent drawing, with whiskers, tail, and other details well defined, but it in no way resembled an apple.

Dr. Elgar, perplexed, bent over a microphone that tapped into the other room's speaker. "Thank you, Wolfgang," he said. "We'll go on to the next one."

Wolfgang looked up expectantly, a shadow of slight disappointment crossing his brow at the lack of response. Then he closed his eyes, nodding, pencil poised over pad again. This time, the assistant's envelope yielded a drawing of a tall skyscraper.

Kelly looked at the drawing and as she looked up her eyes met those of Dr. Dulles. Suddenly, a strange glimmer of recognition flickered and grew stronger as she watched the man settle back against the wall. If she didn't know better, she could swear... But, then, she didn't know—

She sat up straighter, eyes narrowing as she watched Dr. Dulles. Her heartbeat was loud in her chest, a wild but ultimately logical idea forming in her mind. On the monitor, Wolfgang bent over his pad, nodding vigorously, and, with a flourish, produced his next drawing.

A car. The two assistants looked at each other, then back at Dr. Elgar. Dr. Elgar's eyes moved from monitor to target drawing and back. He sighed, and then resignedly pressed the intercom button once more. "Thank you, Wolfgang," he said evenly. "We'd like to do a third, if it's all right with you..." He waited for the psychic to nod, then sat back in his chair. "It's odd," he remarked to one of the assistants. "He was doing so well at first."

"It's not the Chrysler Building, is it?" asked Dr. Dulles, leaning over the desk to get a look at the drawing of the skyscraper. "I mean, that could account for the car—if he's drawn the proper make."

Dr. Elgar gave him a withering stare. One of the assistants chuckled. Kelly put her pad down. Staring at the bearded man, her heart suddenly seemed to be lodged in her throat.

"Dr. Elgar, would you be kind enough to allow me a small experiment?" Dr. Dulles asked.

"Well, I—this is highly... that is," Dr. Elgar stuttered uncertainly.

"Professor Landau has assured me you wouldn't mind."

Exasperated, Dr. Elgar nodded, his lips set tightly. Dr. Dulles turned to the assistants. "Let's do without a drawing altogether this time," he said. "Perhaps Mr. Lang is re-

Under His Spell   163

ceiving images... from other sources... that are conflicting with those the two of you are sending."

The two assistants paused, looked to Dr. Elgar, then shrugged. The doctor rubbed his chin, then sighed, bending over the intercom. "We're opening the third envelope, Wolfgang," he said at length.

On the monitor, the psychic closed his eyes, pen poised over pad once more. Kelly looked to Dr. Dulles. He was still leaning against the wall, not even watching the monitor, his expression unfathomable. Kelly's eyes traveled over him from head to foot, her lips set tightly in grim appraisal.

Wolfgang was squinting, his brow furrowed. It was taking him longer this time. But at last he drew something on the pad, embellished it, concentrated again, then drew another figure on the pad. He considered, thought hard, then slowly brought the paper up for the camera's inspection.

He had drawn what appeared to be a knife, and next to it, a piece of something—metal? glass?—that had a jagged edge.

Dr. Elgar cleared his throat, pausing uncertainly over the intercom. Then he pressed the button. "That will, uh, suffice, Wolfgang, thank you. We'll... Hold on a moment."

He turned to one assistant, indicating he should unbolt the doors to allow Wolfgang entrance, then looked expectantly at Dr. Dulles.

"Interesting," said Dr. Dulles, meeting the other scientist's gaze. "Was anyone here concentrating on either of those particular images?"

The men shook their heads. Dr. Dulles glanced at Kelly, who returned his look with a mute stare. The second door was unbolted now, and Wolfgang came bouncing excitedly into the room. He stopped short, though, when he looked to his right and found someone else in Fritz's place.

"Yah?" he asked Dr. Elgar uncertainly. "What—what is...?"

"I think we have a few... misses," Dr. Elgar said slowly. "The last, uh, drawing—"

Wolfgang shook his head vigorously, his eyes darting around the room. He appeared to be sweating harder. "I get," he began, biting his lower lip. "I got," he corrected himself. "No...image. I got...a..." He paused, perplexed, searching for the proper phrase. "Word," he said at last, nervously scanning the scientists' faces.

"What word?" asked Dr. Elgar.

"I..." Wolfgang cleared his throat. "Where is Fritz?"

"He had to step out for a moment," said Dr. Dulles congenially, leaving his perch by the wall to approach the psychic face to face. "But perhaps you could tell us the word that you...heard?"

Wolfgang stared at him, then nervously flipped the pages on his pad. He held up the image of the knife and jagged edge. *"Was ist..."* he murmured. "Ah, what, you say, what...cuts...you say, *wie sagt man—sharf?"*

"Sharp," Kelly said dryly, and stood.

Wolfgang looked at her. She read the fear in his eyes, and for the first time in her pursuit of the charlatan, she felt a twinge of pity for him. *"Sharf,"* he repeated with a nervous smile. "That is, yes, you say—sharp?"

"Bingo," said Dr. Dulles, with a tight-lipped smile, and he removed his glasses. Then, as the men flanking him stared in astonishment, he removed his beard, wincing as the gummy strands pulled at the skin of his bare cheeks. "As in Julian Sharpe."

Kelly was glad she didn't understand German. Because judging from the harsh tirade of fierce invectives Wolfgang and Fritz hurled at her and the former "Dr. Dulles" when they met briefly in Professor Landau's office, she was being cursed with colorful invention.

Before the two disgruntled and disgraced men left, Fritz also gave a brief speech in English, promising lawsuits, berating the institute for slander and trickery, and ultimately attempting to discredit the United States government. Dr. Elgar, though indignant at having been the victim of deception from both sides, took the whole matter rather gracefully. When Wolfgang and Fritz had been ushered out, he grudgingly congratulated Julian on a job shrewdly managed.

"The device is a small metal disc," Julian explained,

Under His Spell 165

holding up the flat silver cylinder for them to see. "It functions as a sort of contact microphone. When you put it against a metallic surface and tap on it, that tap is received at the other end by a receiving disc, much in the way telegraph typing functions, only at a micro-chip level. Any electronics store worth its hardware could put one of these together, given the right instructions."

"Wolfgang didn't have such a disc on him," Dr. Elgar reminded him.

"No, not once the jig was up," Julian said wryly. "He disposed of it somehow, and fast. But during the testing, he undoubtedly had it either lodged in one ear or stuck behind it."

"But . . . how was he able—" Dr. Elgar began.

"You took Fritz on a tour of the premises, didn't you?" Kelly asked him. The scientist nodded, frowning. "Well, Fritz cased the room, and planted the disc on the wall somewhere . . . I guess they've used the device before."

"Undoubtedly," Julian chimed in. "So, this afternoon, I observed Fritz tapping quietly on the wall's surface—simple words in simple Morse code. And that's what I did myself, after a little help from my German dictionary." He smiled.

"So he really did 'hear' the words *cat* and *car*." Dr. Elgar sighed, shaking his head. "Just as he did the others that Fritz transmitted . . ."

"Jonathan," Professor Landau told him in a kindly tone, "there was no way you could have foreseen—"

"But the other things the man has done, under controlled testing!" Dr. Elgar exclaimed. "For example, the way he caused a compass needle to move by merely staring at it, with no physical contact—he had no magnets in his hands, I can assure you—"

"Did you check his mouth?" Kelly interrupted, and as the befuddled doctor stared at her, she felt Julian's eyes on her, too. "He could have easily concealed a small magnet between lip and teeth," she continued. "It's a fairly routine magic technique."

Professor Landau shook his head. "It's hard to believe a man would concoct such elaborate ruses . . ."

"I'm sure Mr. Sharpe would be happy to demonstrate more of them for you," Kelly said dryly, getting up from her seat. "He's an expert on ruses. As for me, I've got a plane to catch. So if you gentlemen will excuse me—"

She said her good-byes quickly, avoiding Julian's watchful eyes, thinking only of escape. Being in the same room with him and playing the cool professional was possible only for so long. As she hurried from the office, she was aware of Julian rising from his chair. Once outside in the corridor, she nearly broke into a run, desperate to reach the open air. She wasn't about to let herself be ensnared in any more treacherous illusions.

Chapter 9

THE PARKING LOT was vast. Kelly stalked resolutely along the sidewalk path in front of the institute, trying to remember where, precisely, she had parked her rented car.

Her heart was pounding furiously, and she was trembling, she realized, as she walked. Masking her emotions while she'd been inside the little testing room and the professor's office had taken a tremendous effort. But she'd been determined to show nothing—firstly, so as not to interfere with Julian's charade, and secondly, so as not to let that insufferable louse know that he had any effect on her at all.

Now, if she could just make a clean getaway... There was the car, a red compact at the end of the row ahead.

"Kelly!"

She froze only a scant moment in her stride, then walked on.

"Kelly—wait up!"

She didn't acknowledge the sound of his voice, her eyes glued to the car across the expanse of asphalt ahead of her. She heard the footsteps behind her, then walked faster—but Julian's firm grip on her wrist stayed her stride at last. She turned to face him then, her eyes blazing.

"What do you want?" she asked tersely.

He met her defiant gaze straight on, not letting go of her. "I want to talk to you," he said simply. "Why are you running away?"

She stared at him, incredulous. "Why am *I*? After you walked out on me without the slightest hesitation—"

"There was plenty of hesitation involved," he said evenly.

"Although I will admit I was pretty angry. If we'd been on better terms that night—"

"Better terms?" She pulled her arm away angrily. "You bought that ticket in New York, didn't you? Apparently you were planning to ditch me from the start!"

"I wasn't planning on ditching you, as you put it," he said, his eyes blazing. "I had planned to come out here separately, it's true. I thought it would be easier to infiltrate the institute, with Landau's help, if I was alone. But that was before I got to know you—"

"And that really clinched it, right?" she snapped. "When the going gets tough, the tough take a hike? Swell!"

"Kelly." He frowned, shaking his head. "You're always so quick to condemn me. I was planning to tell you about the institute. But when we had that... unfortunate fight, there was no chance to talk about it!"

"I don't really care," she said angrily. "It was a rotten thing to do."

"And it was rotten of you to make up your mind that I was the worst kind of dishonest bum," he retorted.

"So you figured you'd really seal the issue by leaving me high and dry?"

"I don't consider giving you a prepaid plane ticket leaving you high and dry," he muttered. "And I said I'd contact you here, once I—"

"Well, thanks for the contact," she said stiffly. "Now you've done your good deed, and you've nailed Lang to the wall, so unless there's some other professional matter we need to discuss, I'd like—"

"So we're back to that?" He shook his head ruefully.

"We're back to zero, if you like," she said. "That should suit you fine. It makes everything easy, doesn't it? We can go our separate ways without any messy scenes."

"If you weren't such a hot-headed, stubborn fool," he said angrily, "you'd listen to reason. Why don't you give me a chance to explain—"

"I am listening to reason for once," she retorted. "My own! I knew I shouldn't get mixed up with a man like you, and I was right!"

"A man like me," he repeated darkly. "I guess it's easier for you to think the worst of me."

"Easier than what?"

"Than hearing me out—than trusting me—than believing that I'm in love with you!"

Kelly stared at him. She saw the anger in his eyes muted by a soft earnest plea. But before her heart could be swayed, she hardened herself against the spell she knew his eyes could weave. She looked away, unwilling to let herself be taken in again.

"It's too late," she murmured, staring at the black asphalt. "I took a chance—and I'll admit it was... fun, while it lasted," she said bitterly. "But let's just make it one for the memoirs, okay? I have a life to go back to, to get on with. And so do you. It's silly to think we could fit into each other's world—so let's just say good-bye."

"Kelly," he said, "don't walk away like this. We could make a world of our own—"

But she could feel the tears welling up inside of her again, and she didn't want to cry—to let him see her cry; not now. She shook her head mutely, then turned and headed for the car.

"Kelly..." he called. But she kept walking, focused on getting the keys out of her shoulderbag, with trembling fingers. On opening the car door, just moving resolutely forward, without looking back...

She got into the compact, shut the door, and put the key in the ignition. Julian didn't interfere. But as she pulled the car out of the space, she glimpsed him, a tall, achingly handsome man with his arms folded, watching her leave, his eyes glimmering from the shadowy depths of his face. She bade him a silent farewell, then turned the car around and headed for the highway.

"Well? What did you think?"

Kelly looked up from her desk. An expectant Steve Lipman, *Omnibus*'s staff photographer, was waiting for her to get off the phone. Kelly looked at him blankly, motioning that she'd be off in a moment.

"So the train gets in around nine-fifty," she said into the receiver. "You'll be at the station? Good. Okay, Cal. Thanks—I'll see you then." She hung up and turned back to Steve.

"Leaving us again so soon?" he asked.

"Just for the weekend," she told him. "My brother, Cal, has a share in a house out in East Hampton. I just took him up on his open invitation."

"Well, you have been back a week," he joked. "I can't blame you for being impatient to get out of the city."

Kelly sighed. "It's been a particularly busy week." That wasn't the only reason she was taking flight, of course. But she wasn't about to try to explain to Steve how depressed she'd been, how every day she had to sit in the office working on the Wolfgang Lang article was torturous, how she felt like running, hiding... being alone. Although the loneliness was, ironically, the worst part of it. "Anyway—what did I think of what?"

Steve rolled his eyes. "I guess you've been *really* busy," he said. "So I won't take it personally. The photos, Kelly. Which ones are you using? Or, rather—" He cleared his throat in mock nervousness. "Are you using any of them?"

Kelly's eyes moved to the manila folder at the left-hand corner of her desk. It was right where Penny had left it two days ago. Kelly hadn't gotten around to looking at the photos. Actually, she hadn't been able to bring herself to open the folder. Steven had done a shoot of the Sharpe Brothers in action. And though she knew she had to go through his proofs and pull some stills for the sidebar piece on the magician inserted in the Wolfgang Lang article, she'd put it off, and put it off.

But now it was late Friday afternoon, and looking at the photos was her last task before leaving the office. She'd packed her overnight bag and brought it with her; the last thing she wanted hanging over her head for the weekend was that folder. "Sure, we're using some," she said casually, and she leaned across the desk. Steve snatched it up and pulled out a couple of glossies.

Under His Spell

"These?" he asked eagerly, brandishing them before her face.

Kelly looked. There he was, every devastating inch of him spotlit in clear relief against a blue background. Siegfried floated in the air by his side, and James Sharpe grinned from the foreground, his hand seeming to hold up the standing Julian through a trick of photographic perspective. Kelly tore her eyes from Julian's face, clinically inspecting the frame.

"Nice," she said, and flipped it over, scanning the one beneath.

"Nice?" he echoed, affronted. "It's a masterpiece."

"But I like this one better," Kelly said. This photo had Julian more in the foreground, equal with James, Siegfried leaning over both, a paw on each of their shoulders.

Steve nodded. "It's straighter, I guess. But Julian looks a little out of character there, doesn't he? I mean, he's almost smiling."

Kelly examined the face in the photo a moment, then put both down. "I see what you mean," she murmured. "He usually cultivates an air of brooding mystery, doesn't he?" Of course she would have picked the photo that seemed to capture a side of him she knew, Kelly reflected, over one more in keeping with his public image.

Steve had the folder open in front of her now and was turning over pictures. "Then there's a few others I like," he muttered, pointing at one and then another. Kelly nodded, noting that her hand trembled slightly as she held the photos. This was turning out to be just as hard as she'd feared it would be.

"We'll go with the first one," she announced. "Your first choice."

Steve shot her a look. "You're kidding. Don't you want to argue with me? Kelly, are you getting all mellowed out after just a few days in California?"

Kelly forced a smile. "No, I just think you're right, for once." Abruptly, she pushed the pile of photos away from her—but only succeeded in scattering the topmost pile.

"Sorry," she began. "I'll just—"

She froze, staring down at the photograph now revealed inside the folder. Steve followed her gaze, startled. "What's wrong?"

Kelly cleared her throat. "Where did this photo come from?"

Steve craned his neck to see better. "Oh, that's a bunch of pick-ups Mark Margolies gave me—stuff from their publicity packet."

"Publicity . . . ?" Kelly's voice trailed off. The photo was a copy of one she'd seen in Julian's scrapbook. How could she ever forget the twins, sitting on either side of the costumed magician? But what was a shot like this, which she'd assumed was a candid, doing in a publicity packet? She turned the photo over and suppressed an exclamation as she recognized another shot from the infamous scrapbook: the redhead. "Steve," she said, in what she hoped was a nonchalant tone, "who are all these women?"

"Quite a collection," he acknowledged. "They're stage assistants. That particular batch is culled from an American tour a few years back when the Sharpes were using a bunch of showgirls in their act—it was a one-shot deal, actually, from what their manager told me."

"What do you mean?"

"According to Mark, for their first gig headlining in Las Vegas, he had them hire a bevy of beauties to fill out the act—you know, when in Rome. But apparently after the first weekend, they dropped the ladies. Julian thought they were unnecessary, according to Mark. You know, too showbiz."

"I see," Kelly said slowly. The next photo was familiar, too. In fact, if her memory served her well, there was a photo here to match each and every one she'd seen in Julian's book—no more, no less.

"You planning on running more than one shot?"

Kelly looked up at Steve, her mind preoccupied. "Oh—no, no, we'll go with that trick shot you did. It's perfect by itself."

Under His Spell

"Fine with me, Kelly. May I?" He gestured at the opened folder.

"Oh, sure," Kelly said, relinquishing the photos.

"Boy, you must be in a hurry to leave," Steve remarked, as he tucked the folder under his arm. "I've never seen you give me such an easy time."

"It's a good photo," she said vaguely. "Drop it off with Biff, will you? He's starting the paste-ups on Monday."

"Have a good weekend." Steve left the office. Kelly sat at her desk, staring into space.

How wrong had she been?

Once again, as she had untold times over the past sleepless week, Kelly reran that night in the Colorado lodge in her mind. This time, Julian's angry answers to her accusations took on a new significance. What was it he had said about jumping to conclusions...?

Reeling from the tumult of emotions she worked so hard to keep at bay, Kelly got up, restlessly pacing her office. Maybe she'd reacted too fast, read too much into those pictures—pictures that were apparently not souvenirs of romantic liaisons at all. Still, why hadn't he said so?

You wouldn't have listened, she admitted to herself, with a sickened feeling inside.

Kelly let out a tiny moan of frustration. What did it matter? It was over! She'd been working on herself overtime to put the whole experience behind her, to keep Julian from her mind—even as his face and body filled her dreams, night after night. Damn this article! If only she hadn't opened that folder. She hadn't wanted to think of him at all. Now she was cursed with having to wonder...

Glancing at the clock, she realized she should be getting on her way. Gratefully she cleaned her desk, concentrating on the final mundane details. Then, bag in hand, she headed out. But even in the elevator, the undercurrent of thoughts broke through, catching up with her as she fled.

He hadn't called. That was the real answer, wasn't it? He obviously felt it was as over and done with, as she did. What difference did it make that she'd misjudged him on one count? Why torture herself with what she should have—could have—done, what might have been?

Nonetheless, the depression that had plagued her since her return threatened to pull her even lower as she hit the street, the dull realization that a trip to the end of Long Island was not going to make her feel any better slowing her steps as she looked listlessly for a cab. There was one parked at the curb. Just as she was registering its "Off Duty" sign with a grimace of disappointment, to her amazement its driver turned the sign off, indicating he'd take her.

Gratefully, Kelly let him take her bag and stow it in the trunk. She got inside, and when he climbed back into the driver's seat, told him she was going to Penn Station.

"Through the park okay?" he called through the cloudy plastic divider.

"Fine." Kelly settled back as the cab eased into traffic. When she closed her eyes, the images from Steve's photos danced before her eyes. She saw Julian's face with the hint of a smile, the expression that she knew was usually followed by his fingers playing with the ends of his mustache, as he attempted to hide that smile . . . With an inward groan, she wished the memories away. When she opened her eyes, the summer greenery of Central Park was whizzing by her window in the orange glow of approaching sunset. She tried to concentrate on the scenery, though her mind strayed back to the week before, and the greenery of Indiana; of Nebraska.

Only when the cab turned right coming out of the park, instead of left, was she startled from her reverie. "Hold it!" She tapped anxiously on the plastic behind the driver. "I said Penn Station!"

But the cab was headed uptown, gathering speed as it shot up Central Park West. With a jolt of fear, Kelly banged harder on the divider. This was a New Yorker's paranoid nightmare come true—being kidnapped by a crazed cab driver. "Stop!" she called. "Pull over!"

The cab ran a red light. Kelly was terrified. Just as she was trying to unlock the door, anxiously scanning the streets for signs of police, the driver executed a hairpin U-turn that

Under His Spell

sent her flying back against the seat, and pulled over to the curb with a screech of brakes.

"You maniac!" she exclaimed, trying desperately to get her door open. The driver, impervious to her cries, was out of his seat. As he passed by her window, headed for the trunk, Kelly realized he looked oddly familiar. Heart thumping, she finally managed to figure out the door's lock, and she swung it open as the driver slammed the trunk, her bag in his hand.

"I said Penn Station!" she fumed, climbing out. "Where the hell—Theo?!"

There was no mistaking the curly-haired, wiry short figure of the Sharpes' assistant. Grinning sheepishly, he tipped his baseball cap at her—but he kept moving, swiftly striding into the building he'd parked in front of.

"Theo! What are you—my bag!"

Theo was already disappearing through the front doors of the old stone building. Kelly had no choice but to run after him. In vain, she gestured wildly for the building's doorman to stop the young man with her bag, but he merely nodded pleasantly, then turned away, arms folded, eyes scanning the street.

Feeling somewhat like Alice trailing the White Rabbit, in a world that had suddenly turned topsy-turvy, Kelly ran through the doors. Theo was just stepping into an ornate, old-fashioned elevator. Its curving metal grillwork doors slid shut just as she reached it, but Kelly lunged for the button on the wall.

The doors slid open again. Kelly dashed into the elevator. "Theo—!"

But he was gone. Shocked, Kelly froze in the little cubicle, wondering if she was losing her mind. The elevator was here. So where was—

The doors shut behind her. Kelly whirled around. The little panel on the side had a number of buttons. She jabbed the first. But instead of reopening the doors, it started the elevator in motion. With a strangled oath of frustration, she pushed another button. But the elevator continued its slow, rumbling ascent.

Maybe she'd fallen asleep at her desk, Kelly reflected crazily. This couldn't be happening to her. Impulsively, she pushed another button. This time, the elevator slowed, then creaked to a halt. Kelly stood poised at the doors.

When the doors slid open, she found herself momentarily blinded by a flash of light. When her eyes cleared, she froze in shock. At some dozen or so tables, people sat looking at her, smiling, then began to applaud.

With a gulp of acute embarrassment, Kelly tentatively looked beyond the edge of the door. A smiling man in top hat and tails was extending a black cane in her direction. She looked to her left. A woman in a scanty suit of sequins was smiling, her hand extended as well.

"Fantastic trick!" a man in the front row, a few feet directly below and in front of her, exclaimed to his wife. "I don't know *how* they do it!"

Reacting to her expression of complete bewilderment, the audience began to laugh and cheer. As the applause swelled, Kelly stepped back, desperately groping for the elevator panel. She hit the first button, and to her immense relief, the doors closed in front of her.

Heart pounding, she slumped against the wall to the side of the doors as the elevator began its ascent once more. She had to be dreaming; that was the only explanation. The elevator slowed. Kelly steeled herself for whatever might happen next, instinctively shrinking back against the wall as she waited for the doors to open.

But the doors didn't open. Instead, she felt the wall behind her give way. With a shriek, Kelly stumbled backward.

When she regained her balance, she found herself in the foyer of a splendiferously appointed suite. High-ceilinged, with plush Indian rugs, antique wallpaper and gas-jet lamps, it looked like a richly furnished apartment from the Parisian Belle Epoque.

The door-wall slid shut behind her. Cautiously, Kelly moved forward into the room, noting the exquisite details of design—beveled windows with mahogany and velvet

Under His Spell

armoires beneath them, a sumptuous four-poster bed in the room beyond with a silk canopy above it... and her bag.

It was sitting at the foot of the bed. Dazed, Kelly approached the bed and put a hand out to feel the reassuring contours of her bag. The bedroom was filled with the scent of roses. Looking around her, Kelly realized there were bouquets of red and white roses on every side of the bed. A silver ice bucket stand showed off vintage champagne in a gleaming mound of ice. And on the bed behind her bag was a colorfully wrapped box. She leaned forward to read the little card attached to its bow, and saw, with a jolt of surprised recognition, her own name.

But she could no longer be surprised at anything. Hesitantly, Kelly unwrapped the box. Within was a white, full-length chemise of pure silk, with exquisite, gossamer-lace trim. Unable to resist the beautiful thing, she held it up to her, shaking her head. There was a full-length mirror on the wall opposite the bed. Well, if it was her dream, she could do whatever she wished. Holding the chemise against her body, she approached the mirror, then stood, looking at the reflection.

The mirror swung back. Kelly gasped.

"Well," said Julian Sharpe, "is it the right size?"

His eyes appraised her admiringly as he stood in the shadowy space where the mirror had been. Then he stepped forward, and the mirror swung quietly back into place behind him. "It's a petite," he added. "Like the color?"

Kelly exhaled her held-in breath. Steadily, she met his gaze and slowly lowered the silk gown. "I've been expecting you," she said evenly.

She hadn't, really, but her suspicions had been aroused ever since that strange elevator had unceremoniously delivered her onstage in its first stop. Now she did her best to seem unimpressed, as Julian walked closer, playing with the edge of his mustache, but her pulse and heartbeat rose at the nearness of him, nonetheless.

"And I've been waiting for you." He smiled.

"Well, then, I'm sorry I can't stay," she said, as coolly as she could. "It's been fun, but I have a train to catch."

He shook his head. "Don't worry. Cal knows you've been detained."

"What?" Startled, she stared at him. "You mean, you—he—"

"He knows about this little detour, yes," Julian acknowledged.

"Detour? Kidnapping is more like it," she retorted, bristling at his arrogance.

"It's magic." Julian smiled. "I knew you were thinking about me. You wanted to see me. So I rematerialized you, here."

"Very funny," she said. "But I wasn't thinking anything of the sort. And I came by cab—was *coerced*, is more like it. What is this place, anyway?"

"It's The Magic Hotel, of Manhattan," Julian told her. "A private club that caters exclusively to conjurers and their guests."

So that explained the mysterious goings-on. Kelly turned and strode to the bed, draping the lovely chemise over the opened box. She was filled with a tremulous excitement, her head whirling with a tumult of contrary thoughts and feelings. She hadn't been prepared to see Julian again. Now the heady arousal she always felt when he was close to her threatened to overturn her resolute aloofness.

"I appreciate your going to such trouble and expense," she said, her eyes lingering over the roses, the champagne, and all else. "And I guess I have a grudging respect for your dramatic flair," she said wryly, turning to face him again. "But, Julian—what's the point?"

He stood looking at her with an expression on his face that made her stomach quiver. "I think I love you the best," he mused softly, his eyes glowing with amused affection, "when you're trying so hard to be cool, calm, and collected. That's when I can see the beautiful, vulnerable little girl hiding within those emerald eyes of yours."

His caressing gaze and soft, raspy voice were melting her from the inside out. "Julian," she sighed, "don't..."

Before she could step back, he was closer, grasping her hand in his. "Kelly," he murmured, "I've missed you so. I even let go of all my anger when I realized that living another day without you was just plain impossible."

"*Your* anger?" she asked, trembling as his warm hand gently squeezed hers.

"You were wrong," he said simply. "You were so eager to prove *me* wrong that there was no talking to you."

"I suppose," she said stiffly, coloring beneath his steady gaze. "I know now that those photos . . . weren't—"

He shook his head. "No, they weren't."

"But you lied to me," she said, defiantly pulling her hand away. "You said you were so serious about being with me—that you were changing your ways—and then you went ahead and—"

"I talked to Jim," he interrupted, his eyes narrowing. "That morning at the farm, yes—I dealt with my brother in the best way I know how—which is not to openly provoke a major brawl when I'm on my way out the door! If you remember, my eager eavesdropper, I didn't *agree* to anything with him. Did I?"

Kelly swallowed, feeling the flush in her cheeks. "Well, no, but—"

"All I did was mollify and appease him," Julian went on. "I knew that he'd be mad as hell if I dropped a bombshell in his lap and then blithely rode off to Colorado. Jim really wanted that European tour. And even though I'd already made up my mind to cancel it, I knew that the best way to handle the situation was to come back and talk it all out at length with him when I was done working on the Wolfgang thing with you."

"You mean, you—you lied to your brother—?"

"I stalled him!" Julian exclaimed, exasperated. "Kelly Robbins, when are you going to stop seeing deceit in everything I do?"

Kelly lowered her eyes, chagrined. "I'm sorry, Julian," she murmured. "I'm . . . You must think I'm . . ."

"Scared as a bunny in a top hat, yes," he said wryly. "You're so ready to run for cover at the first sign of masculine betrayal it's ridiculous."

"I'm not scared," she said defensively. "It's—I—"

"Really?" He stepped closer. "Well, I'm about to call your bluff, lady. I've canceled the Sharpe Brothers' tour. Jim and I are on a one-and-a-half-year vacation from the road. What do you think of that?"

"What do I—? Well—" She backed away as he kept coming closer, glowering at her. "I—That's great, I guess, but..."

"You guess? And Mark's already negotiating with a friend of his at a publishing house here in New York for a deal on my magic book. How does that sound to you?"

Kelly took another step back. "That's fantastic," she said uncertainly. "I'm—uh, happy for you—"

"You're happy for *me?* Who do you think is going to help me write it?"

He was converging on her with every sentence. Kelly kept moving backward, toward the windows behind her. "Well, I—if you need help..."

"Help?" He sounded incredulous. "I need *you*, you little idiot—and you need me, whether you want to admit it or not!"

There was nowhere to run at this point. Kelly felt the wooden lip of the window seat at the back of her knees. Before she could protest, Julian took hold of her shoulders and gently but firmly pushed her into the seat. Leaning over her, he grasped her chin in his thumb and forefinger.

"Look, you," he said. "I'm tired of being remote and mysterious and uninvolved—and lonely. I want to be close, open, involved, and intimate—and you're the one I want to do it with."

Kelly looked up at him, feeling her eyes fill with tears. "Oh, Julian," she murmured. "I've been wanting the same things."

"I know," he said softly.

"I've—been wanting to hear you say them," she said, her voice becoming tremulous as the tears threatened to break loose.

"I love you," he said, his fingers gently stroking her cheek. "That's what matters, isn't it? Do you believe me now?"

Under His Spell

Mutely she nodded, a thrill of arousal coursing through her at his touch. "Yes," she whispered. "You don't have to say... anything else. I love you."

His lips came to meet hers. For a breathless moment they savored the sweetness of each other's mouth. Then she clung to him, her arms going up around his neck, and the sobs broke forth. Crying, she nestled in his warm embrace, and he kissed her glistening cheeks.

"Kelly," he murmured at last, kneeling by her. "Do you mean... you're willing to be with me? Whatever the future might bring?"

Sniffling, she nodded again. "I shouldn't have pushed you away," she murmured. "I was so afraid of being hurt again... but I'm too in love with you to be afraid, I guess."

Smiling, he kissed her again. "I'm not going to hurt you."

"I'll... help you with the book," she said softly. "And— and when you do go on the road again... I'll—" She paused, at a loss. "Oh, I don't care!" she cried out recklessly. "We're here now."

His eyes glinted in the last rays of the sun, as the sky over Central Park purpled behind them. "Ah," he said softly. "Those are magic words. That kind of faith could turn a tear into a diamond..."

His finger traced a line beneath her eye, the skin wet with tears. When he held the finger up, something bright glittered before her eyes.

It *was* a diamond. A diamond ring.

"Julian!" she gasped. "What..."

"I want you to marry me," he said quietly. "If you were willing to take the risks, I'm certainly willing to make the commitment. Fair's fair."

His smile broadened as she took the ring from him, holding up the sparkling stone with a whistle of admiration. "It's beautiful," she breathed. "Julian, you didn't have to..."

"Yes, I did," he said. "So what do you say?"

"Say?" Dazed, she looked from the ring to his smiling face. "Oh—yes!" she exclaimed. "Yes—I will!"

"You're sure? You're willing to take on me, my brother, and my leopard, for as long as we all shall live?"

Kelly smiled. "I'm willing," she whispered.

Their lips met again and this time the kiss was longer, deeper, as he eagerly explored the treasure of her mouth. Their lips and tongues tangled in a slippery dance of loving as the first star shone in the dusk outside.

"Kelly," he whispered, when at last they broke apart, "there is one piece of deceitful trickery I have to confess to you."

She stared at him in the gathering darkness. "You're not scaring me." She smiled. "Go on."

"I did bend the key to your front door on purpose that day," he said, his eyes twinkling mischievously. "When you held it up on the key chain first and mentally dismissed it immediately, I guessed that was your house key, so I bent it."

"You—!" She shook a mock fist before his face. "But why?"

"I didn't want you going home," he confessed. "I wanted to ensure that you would end up in my arms."

"Risky business," she murmured. "You might have overestimated your charms."

"Charms?" He shrugged. "No, I had faith in my own magic."

"We're going to have to do something about this annoying abundance of self-assurance you have," she murmured as he chuckled. "But I guess you were right, after all. You've got your insurance."

"That's right," he said. "From now on, your home is in my arms."

"Well, then," she whispered, leaning forward for another kiss, "welcome me home."

QUESTIONNAIRE

1. How do you rate _____
   (please print TITLE)
   - ☐ excellent
   - ☐ good
   - ☐ very good
   - ☐ fair
   - ☐ poor

2. How likely are you to purchase another book in this series?
   - ☐ definitely would purchase
   - ☐ probably would purchase
   - ☐ probably would not purchase
   - ☐ definitely would not purchase

3. How likely are you to purchase another book by this author?
   - ☐ definitely would purchase
   - ☐ probably would purchase
   - ☐ probably would not purchase
   - ☐ definitely would not purchase

4. How does this book compare to books in other contemporary romance lines?
   - ☐ much better
   - ☐ better
   - ☐ about the same
   - ☐ not as good
   - ☐ definitely not as good

5. Why did you buy this book? (Check as many as apply)
   - ☐ I have read other SECOND CHANCE AT LOVE romances
   - ☐ friend's recommendation
   - ☐ bookseller's recommendation
   - ☐ art on the front cover
   - ☐ description of the plot on the back cover
   - ☐ book review I read
   - ☐ other _____

(Continued...)

6. Please list your three favorite contemporary romance lines.
   _____
   _____

7. Please list your favorite authors of contemporary romance lines.
   _____
   _____
   _____
   _____
   _____

8. How many SECOND CHANCE AT LOVE romances have you read? _____

9. How many series romances like SECOND CHANCE AT LOVE do you <u>read</u> each month? _____

10. How many series romances like SECOND CHANCE AT LOVE do you <u>buy</u> each month? _____

11. Mind telling your age?
    ☐ under 18
    ☐ 18 to 30
    ☐ 31 to 45
    ☐ over 45

☐ Please check if you'd like to receive our <u>free</u> SECOND CHANCE AT LOVE Newsletter.

We hope you'll share your other ideas about romances with us on an additional sheet and attach it securely to this questionnaire.

• •

Fill in your name and address below:
Name _____
Street Address _____
City _____ State _____ Zip _____

Please return this questionnaire to:
  SECOND CHANCE AT LOVE
  The Berkley Publishing Group
  200 Madison Avenue, New York, New York 10016

FROM THE PUBLISHERS OF *SECOND CHANCE AT LOVE!*

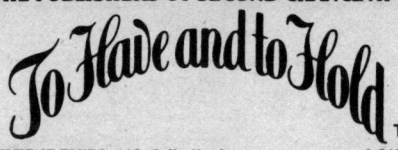

To Have and to Hold
T.M.

___	WHATEVER IT TAKES #15 Cally Hughes	0-515-06942-6
___	LADY LAUGHING EYES #16 Lee Damon	0-515-06943-4
___	ALL THAT GLITTERS #17 Mary Haskell	0-515-06944-2
___	PLAYING FOR KEEPS #18 Elissa Curry	0-515-06945-0
___	PASSION'S GLOW #19 Marilyn Brian	0-515-06946-9
___	BETWEEN THE SHEETS #20 Tricia Adams	0-515-06947-7
___	MOONLIGHT AND MAGNOLIAS #21 Vivian Connolly	0-515-06948-5
___	A DELICATE BALANCE #22 Kate Wellington	0-515-06949-3
___	KISS ME, CAIT #23 Elissa Curry	0-515-07825-5
___	HOMECOMING #24 Ann Cristy	0-515-07826-3
___	TREASURE TO SHARE #25 Cally Hughes	0-515-07827-1
___	THAT CHAMPAGNE FEELING #26 Claudia Bishop	0-515-07828-X
___	KISSES SWEETER THAN WINE #27 Jennifer Rose	0-515-07829-8
___	TROUBLE IN PARADISE #28 Jeanne Grant	0-515-07830-1
___	HONORABLE INTENTIONS #29 Adrienne Edwards	0-515-07831-X
___	PROMISES TO KEEP #30 Vivian Connolly	0-515-07832-8
___	CONFIDENTIALLY YOURS #31 Petra Diamond	0-515-07833-6
___	UNDER COVER OF NIGHT #32 Jasmine Craig	0-515-07834-4
___	NEVER TOO LATE #33 Cally Hughes	0-515-07835-2
___	MY DARLING DETECTIVE #34 Hilary Cole	0-515-07836-0
___	FORTUNE'S SMILE #35 Cassie Miles	0-515-07837-9
___	WHERE THE HEART IS #36 Claudia Bishop	0-515-07838-7
___	ANNIVERSARY WALTZ #37 Mary Haskell	0-515-07839-5
___	SWEET NOTHINGS #38 Charlotte Hines	0-515-07840-9
___	DEEPER THAN DESIRE #39 Jacqueline Topaz	0-515-07841-7
___	THE HEART VICTORIOUS #40 Delaney Devers	0-515-07842-5
___	CUPID'S CONFEDERATES #41 Jeanne Grant	0-515-07843-3
___	PRIVATE LESSONS #42 Katherine Granger	0-515-07844-1
___	HOME FIRES #43 Lee Williams	0-515-07845-X
___	CONQUER THE MEMORIES #44 Jeanne Grant	0-515-07846-8
___	TYLER'S FOLLY #45 Joan Darling	0-515-07847-6
___	PENNIES FROM HEAVEN #46 Jennifer Rose	0-515-07848-4
___	MEMORY AND DESIRE #47 Kate Nevins	0-425-07778-0
___	LOVE NOTES #48 Jane Ireland	0-425-07779-9
___	SWEET COUNTRY MUSIC #49 Vivian Connolly	0-425-07780-2

All Titles are $1.95
Prices may be slightly higher in Canada.

Available at your local bookstore or return this form to:

SECOND CHANCE AT LOVE
Book Mailing Service
P.O. Box 690, Rockville Centre, NY 11571

Please send me the titles checked above. I enclose _____ Include 75¢ for postage and handling if one book is ordered; 25¢ per book for two or more not to exceed $1.75. California, Illinois, New York and Tennessee residents please add sales tax.

NAME _____

ADDRESS _____

CITY _____ STATE/ZIP _____

(allow six weeks for delivery)   THTH #67

Second Chance at Love

___ 0-515-08074-8	**RULES OF THE GAME #218** Nicola Andrews	$1.95
___ 0-515-08075-6	**ENCORE #219** Carole Buck	$1.95
___ 0-515-08115-9	**SILVER AND SPICE #220** Jeanne Grant	$1.95
___ 0-515-08116-7	**WILDCATTER'S KISS #221** Kelly Adams	$1.95
___ 0-515-08117-5	**MADE IN HEAVEN #222** Linda Raye	$1.95
___ 0-515-08118-3	**MYSTIQUE #223** Ann Cristy	$1.95
___ 0-515-08119-1	**BEWITCHED #224** Linda Barlow	$1.95
___ 0-515-08120-5	**SUDDENLY THE MAGIC #225** Karen Keast	$1.95
___ 0-515-08200-7	**SLIGHTLY SCANDALOUS #226** Jan Mathews	$1.95
___ 0-515-08201-5	**DATING GAMES #227** Elissa Curry	$1.95
___ 0-515-08202-3	**VINTAGE MOMENTS #228** Sharon Francis	$1.95
___ 0-515-08203-1	**IMPASSIONED PRETENDER #229** Betsy Osborne	$1.95
___ 0-515-08204-X	**FOR LOVE OR MONEY #230** Dana Daniels	$1.95
___ 0-515-08205-8	**KISS ME ONCE AGAIN #231** Claudia Bishop	$1.95
___ 0-515-08206-6	**HEARTS AT RISK #232** Liz Grady	$1.95
___ 0-515-08207-4	**SEAFLAME #233** Sarah Crewe	$1.95
___ 0-515-08208-2	**SWEET DECEPTION #234** Diana Mars	$1.95
___ 0-515-08209-0	**IT HAD TO BE YOU #235** Claudia Bishop	$1.95
___ 0-515-08210-4	**STARS IN HER EYES #236** Judith Yates	$1.95
___ 0-515-08211-3	**THIS SIDE OF PARADISE #237** Cinda Richards	$1.95
___ 0-425-07765-9	**KNIGHT OF PASSION #238** Linda Barlow	$1.95
___ 0-425-07766-7	**MYSTERIOUS EAST #239** Frances Davies	$1.95
___ 0-425-07767-5	**BED OF ROSES #240** Jean Fauré	$1.95
___ 0-425-07768-3	**BRIDGE OF DREAMS #241** Helen Carter	$1.95
___ 0-425-07769-1	**FIRE BIRD #242** Jean Barrett	$1.95
___ 0-425-07770-5	**DEAR ADAM #243** Jasmine Craig	$1.95
___ 0-425-07771-3	**NOTORIOUS #244** Karen Keast	$2.25
___ 0-425-07772-1	**UNDER HIS SPELL #245** Lee Williams	$2.25
___ 0-425-07773-X	**INTRUDER'S KISS #246** Carole Buck	$2.25
___ 0-425-07774-8	**LADY BE GOOD #247** Elissa Curry	$2.25
___ 0-425-07775-6	**A CLASH OF WILLS #248** Lauren Fox	$2.25
___ 0-425-07776-4	**SWEPT AWAY #249** Jacqueline Topaz	$2.25

Prices may be slightly higher in Canada.

Available at your local bookstore or return this form to:

SECOND CHANCE AT LOVE
Book Mailing Service
P.O. Box 690, Rockville Centre, NY 11571

Please send me the titles checked above. I enclose _____ Include 75¢ for postage and handling if one book is ordered; 25¢ per book for two or more not to exceed $1.75. California, Illinois, New York and Tennessee residents please add sales tax.

NAME _____

ADDRESS _____

CITY _____ STATE/ZIP _____

(allow six weeks for delivery)

SK-41b